By the same author

Historical Fiction

The Hanging Tree
Runaway
Homestead (Runaway Series: Book Two)
Chickadee (Runaway Series: Book Three)
Savage
Where Seagulls Fly (2013 Edition)
Song of the Sea
The Shepherd of St Just

Other Fiction

The Black Rose (short stories)
Eve White
Fey
For Love or Money
Heart's Desire
Love & Other Oddities (short stories)
The Magical Isles Trilogy
Minos
Quiddity (2013 Edition)
The Red Brick Road
Synergy

Other Non-Fiction

Gothic Fantasy: The Films of Tim Burton
My Human Condition (poetry)
Quintessential Tarantino
Twin Flames: Poetry of Love Book I (Kindle only)
Sacred Waters: Poetry of Love Book II (Kindle only)
Night Whispers: Poetry of Love Book III (Kindle only)
Twin Flames: Poetry of Love (paperback compendium edition)
The Writer in Me, The Writer in You

Snow Dancer

By Edwin Page

Curved Brick

First published to Kindle & paperback in 2018
by Curved Brick, UK

Copyright © Edwin Page 2018

No.69

All rights reserved

To Dawn
for the company and the encouragement

&

To my mother, Ellen
for helping with the Swedish translations

Pronunciation of Swedish vowels:
Ä: air
Å: or
Ö: eur (as in secateurs)
It is also the case that a J is commonly pronounced as a Y, so 'hej' becomes 'hey.'

We will be known forever by the tracks we leave behind
(Native American saying)

Tuesday, April 8, 1873

I watched out of the window as Nicky chased a butterfly along the line of the front fence. Waiting for it to settle, he closed on its position with hands at the ready. Each time he drew near, the orange insect took to the wing, moving further away until settling amidst the wildflowers once again.

I smiled as I stood at the open window, the April sun dipping towards the western hilltop behind the house and its warm light bathing the vale. I could hardly believe our son was already seven and would be eight in the fall. The years since your departure had swept by and were a tapestry of ploughing, planting, tending, harvesting, and mending, along with time spent with the Olsens and bringing up our child.

Standing there, I felt you in my heart more strongly than I had in a long time. I knew the love I felt for Nicky was not just mine, it was our love being expressed. Part of you remained and it was the best thing, the most potent thing; love.

My gaze moved inward as Nicky continued to pursue the butterfly, ignoring others that were disturbed by his passage. I pictured your face, softened by the years, but your smile and eyes still vivid.

'I caught it.'

I blinked and looked to Nicky as he raised his cupped hands high in the air, a victorious grin upon his face. You were in his features and his eyes. You had left your mark both on my heart and in our son's likeness.

'Now set it free,' I called back.

'Isn't there a jar I can keep it in, just for a time?'

'Its beauty is in its natural state, as with all things. If you have respect for this, you will let it go.'

Nicky continued to look at me for a moment, his smile fading. He nodded his understanding and stared down at his hands. Opening them a fraction so that he could examine the creature, he mumbled a few words that I could not make out and then released it from captivity.

The butterfly fluttered up. Passing about his head, it settled on his short and tight black curls.

'It is thanking you for letting it go,' I said.

His eyes turned upward as he stood still. The butterfly flexed its wings in the fading sunlight. Taking to the air once again, it flew over the boundary fence and was soon lost to sight.

I tried to see it one last time, eyes narrowed as I sought a flash of orange. Noting something out of place in the distance, my focus readjusted and I looked to the trees on the far side of the vale. A stooped silhouette stood in the gloom, the strand of woodland thick with growing shadow.

It remained motionless and I wondered if it might be the trunk of a tree that had died during the winter, its upper portion having fallen away and rotting in the undergrowth out of sight. Though I could not recall seeing it before, I could not be certain.

My heart leapt as the figure moved. I noted the unmistakable presence of arms at its sides as it passed deeper into the woodland and vanished from sight.

'Anders?' I asked, immediately shaking my head. His posture was straight and his shoulders wider. The figure amidst the trees had seemed bent with age and moved with the likeness of someone lacking agility.

I continued to scan the woods, sure that the figure had been watching the house. More than that, I felt it had been watching us and the thought made me ill at ease, a shiver running through me as the hairs on my arms tingled.

* * *

The sun had been gone for a good hour before Anders and Marie came along the path, though its light still caught on the upper slopes of the eastern hill on the other side of the vale. Marie walked behind her husband with a large dish in her hands, the pie she had promised covered with a chequered cloth to keep the flies off.

I saw them while preparing the table, the white cloth smoothed by my hand as I passed on the way to the door in my traditional buckskin dress. Nicky was seated on the boards before the fire. He was playing a game with a circle of smooth black stones collected from the stream, skipping one over the others to then place it inside the ring as he slowly created a spiral.

'They are here,' I stated as I took hold of the handle.

He turned with a bright expression, immediately rising to his feet and running to join me, the game of patterns forgotten.

I opened the door. 'Anders, Marie, welcome,' I greeted, Nicky pushing by my hip and running to the Swedes.

Anders bent and caught our boy in his arms, raising him up and the two embracing. 'It was only yesterday that I last saw you, but I swear you've grown another inch still. What do you say, Marie?' he asked over his shoulder in his accented voice.

'I say, he'll be taller than us all within the month if that's how fast the boy grows,' she replied with a smile that deepened the shallow lines about her eyes, her long sandy hair tied back with a length of red ribbon and wearing a plain blue housedress.

'That may be true with your good food to encourage his growth,' I responded as they neared, feeling plain in sight of her natural elegance.

'Hej, Chula,' greeted Anders, his mess of blonde hair complimenting his blue eyes and his face filled with strength. He was wearing his usual deep green coat, a pale shirt beneath and braces attached to his corduroys.

I stepped back and he entered with Nicky still held to him, the Olsens and our son sharing a strong bond. Marie pulled up before me and leant forward, kissing me on the cheek.

'Hejsan,' she greeted in her native language, the words meaning 'hello friend.'

'Hej,' I replied in kind.

'Did you get to hoeing the weeds?'

I nodded as she entered and I closed the door. 'With Nicky's help, they will be cleared by the end of the week from both the vegetable patches and fields.'

She walked to the stove that had been bought the previous year, placing the pie beside the hotplate and leaving the covering cloth in place. 'It still carries a little warmth from home,' she said. 'The heating through won't take long.'

'I have some vegetables to go with it.'

'There's plenty mixed in with the chicken,' she replied, looking at the dishes of broccoli and cauliflower resting to the rear of the stove.

'I see you have been playing,' said Anders to Nicky, setting him on his feet.

'You want to play too?'

Anders looked at the stones as he took off his coat, stepping to the hooks beside the door and hanging it up.

'I don't know what I should do,' he responded as Nicky took his hand and led him over.

He sat on the floor before the circle of pebbles and looked up at Anders expectantly. The Swede seated himself cross-legged next to him.

'Will you give me a demonstration?'

'I'll show you what to do,' confirmed Nicky, turning his attention to the collection as Marie and I seated ourselves at the table.

'The cattle are laying in the field,' stated Marie, brushing stray strands of hair from her forehead with a natural flourish.

'Is that important?'

'Anders says there's cold weather yet to come.'

I glanced out of the window, the mildness making it hard to believe her prediction.

'I know what you're thinking, but he has not been wrong before.'

I looked across at her, still dubious, but seeing it as no great matter to be discussing further. 'How do your livestock fare?'

'The cows were worried by coyotes last night, but Anders saw to scaring them away,' she replied. 'He fired his shotgun into the air and we hope that's the last of them.'

I glanced at Nicky and Anders to make sure the boy's attention was elsewhere. 'I saw something today,' I stated quietly, leaning towards her.

'What was it?' she enquired, her curiosity piqued by my behaviour.

'Someone was in the woods on the other side of the vale.'

'A trapper?'

I shook my head. 'I do not think so.'

'What were they doing?'

'They appeared to be watching the house. If I had to guess, I would say they were old. They had a stoop and the way they walked suggested great age.'

She glanced out of the window as she thought about what I had said. 'And you have no idea who it may have been?'

'The shadows were too deep.'

'Maybe a vagabond passing through,' she pondered, turning back to me. 'He may have been thinking of calling to ask for food and shelter. There are plenty who wander the states without home or work since the war. Some are old soldiers and others were once slaves.'

I nodded, but said nothing, thoughts turning to the few waifs and strays that I had come across. The fighting had ended eight years previous and there had been at least three occasions when those left with nothing as a result of the conflict and its repercussions had passed through the vale.

'Is everything all right?'

I blinked and looked over at Marie. 'Sorry. I was faraway.'

'I was asking how the chickens are? You found one dying on the floor of the coop.'

'Pecked to death by the others,' I said with a nod. 'There have been no more since,' I replied, recalling how the chickens had begun to pick on one of their own, pecking away the feathers from its rear and finally bringing it near to death, the poor bird unable to rise and breathing heavily. I had wrung its neck, the body now hanging in the pantry.

'And they still lay?'

'They do. There has been no change in that,' I replied. 'I have some eggs for you in a bowl, if you would like them.'

'We have plenty, but thank you.'

'Look what Anders has made,' said Nicky.

We looked to the spiral on the floorboards, five arms curling in towards a central stone.

'Just from hopping them over each other,' said Nicky, clearly impressed.

'And if we hop the middle stone out to the edge, we can begin making the circle again,' stated Anders.

I rose from my seat and checked the heat rising from the hotplate by holding my hand above. Finding it warm enough, I took the cover from the nearby dish and put the pie in place. I took a couple of logs from the pile to the right and opened the front, placing them inside.

'There,' I said, turning to the others. 'It should not be too long.'

* * *

I rested my knife and fork on my plate and leant against the back of the chair. Anders was still busy eating his second helping, Nicky having followed suit, holding the Swede in high esteem and often copying him. He was struggling with his small extra portion, chewing slowly and forcing it down as he glanced at Anders.

'You do not have to eat it all,' said the Swede, noting the boy's dilemma. 'I'm feeling full and may have to leave some.'

'You think you will?' asked Nicky.

Anders set his knife down and patted his stomach. 'I think I'm going to have to leave what remains. One more bite and I may burst,' he replied with a smile.

'I feel the same,' said Nicky, putting his cutlery down and holding his distended belly, a look of mild relief upon his youthful face.

'I hear your schooling is going well,' stated Anders.

'Ishki says I am better at writing than she was at my age,' replied our son proudly.

'And it is true,' I said before turning to Marie. 'I had better wash your dish before you leave.'

'I can do that when we return home,' she replied.

'It is the least I can do. After all, you went to the effort of making the pie and brining it here.'

I stood and turned my back on the table, picking up the pie dish and taking it to the bucket resting on the floor to the right of the stove. Crouching, I washed it clean with the cloth that had been hanging over the side.

Stepping to the table, I set the dish down, its dampness seeping into the tablecloth.

'Thank you,' said Marie with a tired smile. 'I think it is time for us to leave.'

'Already,' responded Nicky with obvious disappointment.

'We have much to do tomorrow,' she stated, stifling a yawn as she got to her feet.

'I have a sponge cake with strawberry jam filling,' I stated. 'I thought we could all have a small slice.'

Anders looked hopefully at his wife, but she shook her head. 'There is lots to do and we should get some sleep in readiness,' he said regretfully.

'I will cut you both a slice and you can have it tomorrow.'

I went to the dresser and opened one of the doors at the bottom, taking the cake tin from inside. Placing it on the table, I removed the lid, the Olsens looking at the yellow cake and Nicky craning his neck to peer in.

'Did you make it?' asked Marie.

I shook my head as I returned to the dresser and opened the top left drawer, taking out a clean knife. 'It was from my sister,' I replied over my shoulder as I took four plates down from the shelves above.

'Are you sure you will not have some here?' I asked, setting the plates down, my tone and expression hopeful.

'Please stay,' pleaded Nicky.

The Olsens shared a look.

'I think we can stay a little longer,' conceded Marie, seeing her husband's wish to remain and settling back down.

My gratitude for having such friends came to the fore. They had been steadfast throughout the years I had known them and our relationship had become close. They doted on Nicky, often bringing him a gift and always willing to give him their time and attention.

I cut four slim slices and handed them out. 'There is plenty if any of you want more,' I said, retaking my seat as Nicky eagerly tucked into his slice, crumbs about his mouth and a smear of jam upon his chin.

Wednesday, April 9, 1873

I woke to the dawn light. Stretching and wiping a tear from my cheek, I raised my head and looked over to Nicky. Our son was still sound asleep, the large meal the night before deepening his slumber. He and Anders had tackled second slices of the cake, both managing to eat them despite supposedly having been full after the main course.

I rose, taking care to put on my buckskin dress and britches as quietly as possible, Nicky murmuring in his sleep and turning to face the wall. Going over to him once I was done, I bent beside his cot and pulled his cover up to keep him from the morning chill before kissing his cheek.

I made my way out into the hall and glanced down at the slight gap that ran across the passage, marking where the newer boards began. The house had been extended to the rear, the expansion helping to dispel Coop's imprint and giving us a storeroom and two bedrooms, though Nicky had recently moved into mine due to recurring nightmares.

Walking into the main room, I recalled how I had been woken by his screams a couple of weeks previous. Lighting a lantern and running in, I had found him quaking beneath his covers, knees pulled to his chest and eyes wide. He had dreamt of an old man dancing before a fire, his grin filled with wickedness as shadows moved upon his whiskered face and the thump of his boots reverberated to the bone. The image of Coop jigging had come to mind, though I had no idea how our son could have known of it.

The same dream had come three nights in a row, always resulting in Nicky waking with screams. On the third occasion the dream had ended with him being caught in a bear trap as the old man loomed over him with evil intent glinting in his eyes.

For the first few nights after that, he had joined me in my bed, tossing and turning through the early hours as dreams continued to disturb him. Able to get little sleep due to his activity, I had decided to move his bed into my room.

Though we had only shared the room a short while, I had grown accustomed to having our son nearby. If I woke during the night, the sounds of him sleeping would lull me back into slumber and when I rose in the mornings, it was a pleasure to be greeted by his restful expression, his nightmares receding as the days passed.

I went to the stove and opened the right-hand door, picking up the poker and disturbing the ash so that it fell through the gaps in the grate. Placing some kindling inside, I struck a match and lit it, watching a moment as the flames took. Putting larger timbers on top, I closed it and slid out the tray filled with ash beneath.

Going to the door, I slipped on my moccasins, which I had hand stitched and dyed deep red. Vacating the house, I went along the path and out of the gate, the hinges squeaking slightly and followed by the bump of wood against wood. My breath was captured in mist as I passed around the trees which had been mere saplings upon our arrival. The patch of suckers had been thinned, but those that had been left were now twenty feet tall, their growth never failing to impress. All were freshly budded and vibrant green, the air rich with the scent of spring vitality.

The ruined barn rested ahead, but I paused beyond the trees to add the ash in the pan to the pile already resting there. Leaving the pan on the grass beside, I continued on in order to visit your final resting place.

I entered through the old doorway, the walls more tumbledown than they had been when you still lived. The interior was thick with vegetation apart from an area two feet wide about your grave where I kept the grass cut short. Walking along the well-worn trail to your side, I settled upon my knees on the right-hand side, looking to the stones and resting my hand upon the topmost. Its cold dampness was in contrast to the warmth in my heart as I looked up to the remains of the window. The sun was approaching the top of the eastern side of the vale, its light already resting on the western slopes.

I waited, a solitary bee flying past, its flight low and lazy in the morning coolness. Glancing over my shoulder, I saw the tip of the sun rise over the brow of the eastern hill, its first beams captured in my eyes as I knelt, the damp from the trimmed grass seeping through my britches. The wall and grasses opposite my position were bright beyond the shadow cast by the hill, the latter heavy with dew and sparkling in the sunlight.

'Chi-hollo-li,' I stated, the words meaning 'I love you' in Chickasaw.

Such was the way by which I began each day, only two briefs spells of sickness having seen me unable to make my pilgrimage to your resting place. Come rain or shine, I made my way to the barn. Sometimes I took posies of wildflowers and sometimes Nicky would accompany me, if he was wakeful and willing. He sensed the sadness contained within that old ruin and was often disinclined to join me.

'Nicholas,' I whispered, taking a deep breath as I stared at the slick stones.

Removing my hand, I slowly got to my feet and turned. The warmth of the sun upon my face, but the lower half of my body in shadow, I turned away and made my way back out of the building.

* * *

We passed south along the vale. A light mist lingered in the shadow cast by the eastern hill, hanging over the grassland and woven between the trees, though the house was bathed in sunshine. Nicky held my hand, yawning and still subdued by his recent wakefulness. I had changed into a housedress such as the white folk wore and topped it with a hooded cloak in readiness for a visit to the settlement, the need to blend in forcing me to don the clothes which I found so unsavoury.

We made our way around the end of the hill, passing into the sunlight and both squinting against the brightness. Turning west, we made for the Olsens' farm, where our son spent every Monday and Wednesday morning while I visited with Esther.

'Will you be getting another cake today?' asked Nicky as the sunshine burnt away the last of his weariness.

I smiled and glanced at him. 'We have not finished the other as yet.'

'But it won't last until next Monday,' he stated. 'If she gives you another it will see us through.'

'We will see. It may be she has made some of that seeded bread you like or maybe she has made nothing at all,' I replied, knowing that Essy had to be careful how much she gave to us for fear of discovery.

'Uncle Anders has promised to take me out on the horse when he's done with tending the livestock,' he stated happily, using the honorary title that had been earned over the years, referring to Marie as 'Auntie.'

'You be careful.'

'He'll be riding with me,' he replied.

'Would you like to visit Auntie Esther with me next week?'

He shrugged. 'I don't mind.'

'You ought to come with me sometime soon. You have not been for over a month.'

'Would she make another cake if I did?'

I chuckled. 'I am sure that if I asked her to, she would bake one to celebrate seeing her nephew.'

'With strawberry jam?' He looked up at me, his eyes sparkling with desire as he licked his lips.

'With strawberry jam,' I confirmed, squeezing his hand.

There was an unmistakable spring in Nicky's step as we continued, the prospect of spending time at the Olsens' and the possibility of another cake in the near future combining to put him in high spirits. By the time we crossed the expanse of grassland south of their farmstead, he was almost skipping, drawing me along in his wake as the birds sang their springtime chorus.

We approached the front door, hearing their rooster call to the rear of the property.

'Can I knock?'

I nodded in response to our son's request and he released my hand. Going to the door ahead of me, he banged on it loudly, his excitement making him over-zealous.

Marie glanced out of the open window to the right, hands white with flour. She waved and smiled. 'Come in.'

Nicky opened the door and entered hurriedly. 'Is Uncle Anders here?'

'He's seeing to the chickens,' she replied as I stepped in.

'Aren't you going to greet Auntie Marie properly?' I chided.

'Good morning, Auntie Marie,' he said quickly.

'Can I go help Uncle Anders?' He looked at me expectantly.

I glanced at Marie, who nodded. 'Go on then,' I replied, 'but be sure not to pester him about the horse riding,' I called after him.

'I won't,' he replied as he ran past the window and around the side of the house.

I looked to Marie and shook my head. 'I am sorry,' I stated.

'There is nothing to be sorry for,' she replied, returning to the dough resting on the table before the window. She waved away a fly and continued with her kneading.

I watched her for a moment, her knuckles sinking into the dough. Feeling a swell of emotion, I stepped over and gave her a kiss on the cheek. 'Thank you.'

'For what?' she asked in mild surprise.

'Being you,' I responded. 'I do not know what would have become of us without you both.'

'We have done nothing more than you have done for us,' she replied, taking a pinch of flour from the paper parcel beside her and sprinkling it over the dough.

'What have I done?'

'You have helped us here when needed, given food when you have it spare and shown great hospitality,' she stated.

Her smile faded a little as she looked to me fondly. 'You have also given us a son.'

We looked into each other's eyes a moment and I put a hand to her back. 'I am sorry you have yet to be blessed with your own children.'

'It's God's will,' she replied simply.

I made no comment, balking slightly at the reference to the Olsens' Christianity. By and large, my experience of that religion had been of domination, cruelty and intolerance. Marie and Anders had softened my opinion, as had your faith, my love. I had come to see the Great Spirit and God as one and the same; merely the way that different cultures expressed the same essential presence.

'Do you want to have lunch here when you return for Nicky?' she asked, blinking away tears that had arisen in response to thoughts relating to their lack of offspring.

'That would be a kindness,' I replied, my heart reaching out to Marie in sight of her sadness.

'There'll be fresh bread,' she stated.

I stood watching as she folded the dough on itself a few times, wishing there was something to be said that would reduce her pain. 'I had best be on my way or the morning will be all but done by the time I get there,' I said, finding no words that would penetrate deep enough in order to bring healing.

'See you when you return,' she responded with a glance and smile, the expression lacking vigour.

I turned and made my way to the door.

'You can leave it open. The day is a fine one, despite the cattle lying down,' she stated, trying to lighten her mood with a touch of humour.

I walked out of the house and paused on the porch, lifting my face to the sun and closing my eyes. Taking a breath, I headed south, hearing our son's laughter arise from the rear of the property as an orange winged butterfly flitted by.

* * *

I pulled the hood of my cloak over my head when the reservation buildings came into view. There had been numerous new constructions during the time I had been living in the vale, many by white folk wishing to sell their wares to the Chickasaw Nation. New stores had sprung up and the administration of the reservation had changed hands. Agent Jackson had moved on and been replaced by a man named Thompson, or so my sister told me. Inki had let my actions be known at a gathering of the elders soon after I had left and I was an outcast from the Nation, meaning my time in the town was limited and anonymous by necessity.

Keeping my head bowed and face concealed in the shadow of the hood, I made my way along the main street. My boots sank into the mix of mud and manure, heavy spring rains having left large puddles in the ruts.

I looked to the ground, my steps hurried as I made my way to an alley leading to the left. Passing into its confines, I felt some relief, the chance of discovery diminishing.

Moving through its shadows, I inadvertently kicked a bottle left lying on the ground. It spun and splashed into a brown puddle, its stained label revealing that it was Tennessee whisky.

Reaching the end of the alley, I passed across another wide street into a side passage. Going to the door at its far end, I knocked twice. Waiting a moment, I knocked once and then twice more.

I dared to lift my head in order to look back to the street, seeing a cart pass by, the driver intent upon the view ahead. The creak of hinges drew my attention back to the door and I found Esther standing before me, rounded by the years that had passed and made homely by her life as a housewife and mother.

She held a finger to her lips and stepped back so that I could enter. Going inside, she quickly closed the door behind me.

Waving for me to follow, she led the way out of the kitchen through a back door. Passing across a courtyard, we went up a small set of steps to the granary. Entering, my nostrils were filled with the scent of grain. There were two stalls to either side, those on the right empty and the others containing a few sacks of wheat and barley remaining from the previous year's harvest. In autumn all the stalls were filled with piles of grain, the gap beneath the building allowing the air to circulate and helping to dry them out.

Essy stepped to me, taking me into a tight embrace. 'Sister,' she whispered as we held each other close.

'Sister,' I responded.

We parted and she moved to sit on the low wooden wall that fronted the stalls on the right. 'We best keep quiet. Delphi is set to cleaning the bedrooms,' she said, referring to her mother-in-law.

'Do you want me to leave?'

She shook her head and reached out to take my hand. 'How is Nicky?'

'He is well and will be riding with Anders while I am visiting with you.'

'Will it be his first time?'

I nodded. 'He has requested another cake like the one you gave me on Monday.'

'I'm glad he liked it.'

'How goes everything here?'

'Delphi is coming uninvited more and more often. I think she doesn't believe I can keep the house clean. She's always scrubbing and brushing.'

'She may just be lonely since her husband died,' I suggested. 'How is Inki?' I asked, struggling to say the words.

'He seems to age more each time I see him,' she replied regretfully.

I nodded. Ishki had passed away only months after I had left the farm. There had never been any contact with Inki and when Esther had once suggested visiting with me, he had refused to even listen.

'How are the children?'

'Constance and Robert are looking forward to meeting their new sibling,' she stated, glancing down at the bump that was just starting to show.

I gave another nod, a touch of sadness arising in response to the names she had chosen for her children, as it always did. I had hoped she would pick traditional Chickasaw names, but she had long since left that past behind or, at least, had been coerced to do so.

'Esther?'

We both turned to the door at the sound of her mother-in-law's croaky voice.

Essy held her finger to her lips. Picking up an empty sack draped over the stall wall, she stepped to the door as I moved out of view. 'Here, Delphi,' she said, opening it to find the cranky old woman coming across the courtyard as she grumbled to herself.

'I thought you were set to changing the sheets,' stated Delphi, stopping at the bottom of the wooden steps.

'I decided it best to bake some fresh bread. It's better to be made in the morning so there is time for it to rise before lunch.'

'There's bread in the bin.'

'I found some mould,' responded Esther.

I watched Delphi through a crack in the wall, keeping back so my face wouldn't be seen. She frowned, the wrinkles to either side of her mouth deep and hinting that it was her most common expression.

'Just cut it off. My son wouldn't want you wasting food,' she stated. 'The wasteful girl knows nothing of hardship,' she grumbled afterwards, habitually voicing her thoughts and totally unaware that she did so.

'The old bread will be given to Teddy for pig feed and he always gives carrots or beets in exchange,' replied Esther, referring to Nathan's brother.

Delphi regarded her a moment. 'Got an answer for everything, she has. Never wrong and never learning from her elders,' she grumbled. 'You'd better get to it,' she said to my sister. 'There are plenty of chores that need seeing to.'

'I won't be long,' said Esther.

Hesitating, Delphi then went back into the house, her mumbles beyond the ability to be heard as she shook her head, greying hair swaying with the motion. The door shut and Essy listened to the old woman's departure before turning to me.

'You'd best leave out the back,' she said with a glance at the wide door at the rear of the granary.

'Already?' I asked in disappointment.

'Delphi will be like a hawk until I'm busy with the chores she thinks I should be doing.'

I sighed, but made no protest.

'Hold this open,' she said, holding the empty sack out to me.

Taking it, I opened the top and held it with its bottom to the floor as she readied herself to pour grain from a half sack she lifted out of the nearest stall. It streamed out, the sackcloth going taut as it filled.

'You can be taking that one with you,' she said when the sack was a third full. 'Get me another empty one so I can take some into the house to grind for bread.'

'Why don't you just use flour?' I asked, stepping to where other sacks were draped on the right-hand dividing wall.

'She's going to be expecting me to have grain now that she knows I've been out here. We should be thankful she didn't take a look in the cupboards. She'd have found there's plenty of flour left.'

I held the second sack at the ready and she poured enough grain in so as to make a good sized loaf. Placing the near empty sack back into the stall atop the others gathered there, she dusted of her hands.

'I'm sorry your visit has to be cut short,' she said, noting my downcast expression. 'Maybe you could come by on Friday as well this week. See if you can bring Nicky.'

'Will you bake a cake?' I asked, forcing a smile.

'I'll see what I can do. Nathan's sense of smell seems more acute when it comes to sweet things. Last time I had to bake two because I was sure he'd sniff out my activity. Sure enough, he asked after the baking as soon as he came in from the fields.'

'You are a good wife to him,' I stated, 'and a good mother to the children.'

'That's not what he'd say if he ever caught us, considering your position and all,' responded Essy, regretting her words as soon as she had uttered them, her expression falling. 'Sorry, I shouldn't have mentioned it.'

'I have no position. To the Nation I am nothing,' I stated, 'but it is something I have lived with for a good many years, so there is no need for apology.'

'I would that I could change things.'

'What is done, is done. I made my choice when Nicholas and I ran away from the farm,' I said, not wishing to discuss the matter, which had been raised by my sister upon every visit in the early years of my life in the vale, but which she had taken to avoiding in recent times.

She regarded me sadly. 'I would do anything to have you and Nicky join us at the table, for him to meet his cousins and for all of us to be a family without fear of discovery or reprisal.'

'As would I,' I admitted, 'but we have to live the lives we have and take responsibility for the choices that have moulded them. I knew the consequences, but love was stronger.'

'You did love him, didn't you?' she said, her words more a statement than a question.

'I still do and my heart remains his until my dying day.'

She smiled sadly at me. 'Then maybe everything is as it should be. God is love, so you followed His path when you followed your heart. I can see no wrong in that.'

'You are the only one,' I responded, gathering the top of the sack together in readiness to leave and testing its weight.

'The others only know what father told them. They see the surface of things, not the depths that moved you to act. It is in those depths that God dwells, Nora,' she stated, using the Christian name I had been forced to take at school.

'We once called it the Great Spirit,' I said without looking at her, trying not to become agitated by her words and her transformation into the semblance of those that had conquered and persecuted our people.

'If we cling to the past, we cling to what's gone, not what is,' she stated.

'Let us not argue about this again,' I responded, lifting the sack onto my shoulder.

She looked at me with a frown but said nothing more, all too familiar with my stubbornness and wish to keep at least some of our traditions alive despite the shadow that had fallen over all native peoples. Reaching forward, she lifted my hood over my head.

'Take care, Sister,' she said regretfully.

I wanted to lower the sack, to step forward and take her into my arms, but the hardness within me that had arisen as a result of our exchange kept me in place. 'I will call on Friday,' I stated with a nod of parting, turning to the rear door.

Esther followed behind, leaning past me to pull back the bolt.

'Till Friday.' She opened the door to the track and fields beyond, the breeze stirring the edge of my hood and brushing against my cheeks.

'Farewell.' I walked out, passing down the steps to the grass and mud. Turning, I looked up as she closed the portal, my last image being of the deep frown upon her face.

Following the track to the right, I reached an alley that took me into the heart of the town. Shoulders hunched and filled with tension as I made my way along the streets, I kept my head bowed and set my thoughts to Nicky and home.

'Miss?' It was a man's voice and arose from a few yards behind me.

I quickened my pace and stepped over a pile of fresh horse manure as a couple of Chickasaw farmhands walked by in the opposite direction, their britches covered in mud and black hair cut to the shoulders.

'Miss?' This time the voice was closer and I could hear footsteps behind.

The touch of a hand upon my shoulder gave me a start and brought me to an unwilling halt. The man walked around to stand in front of me, ducking his head to look up at my face as it remained largely concealed by the hood.

I looked out at him nervously and was immediately struck by his eyes. They sparkled in the shadow cast by the brim of his dark hat. In their depths was compassion and intelligence, my stomach fluttering in response. His face was strong, with high cheekbones and a firm jaw line. He wore a pale green shirt with braces and I judged him to be in his late-twenties. His long black hair tumbled loose about his wide shoulders and he was one of the Nation to which I still felt I belonged, but which had cast me out.

He blinked as if taken aback. 'Um…,' he began, words temporarily escaping him.

'What do you want?' I asked bluntly, raising my head slightly and irritated by my reaction to his appearance.

'I just thought to tell you that grain is falling from a tear in the sackcloth.'

'Grain?' I asked in momentary confusion.

'From the sack over your shoulder,' he clarified.

Feeling foolish at not having understood, I felt a blush rise to my cheeks. 'Thank you,' I stated, taking the sack from my shoulder and cradling it against my stomach, a hand covering the rip.

Stepping around him, I continued along the street.

'Wait!' he said after I had taken a couple of steps.

I turned.

'I haven't seen you here before,' he stated. 'Have you just moved?'

I shook my head. 'I must be on my way.'

'At least let me know your name,' he said. 'After all, I did save your grain from emptying.'

'Chula,' I answered, surprising myself.

'Fox,' he stated with a smile.

I began to walk away after a hesitation, surprised that he knew the meaning of my name.

'My name's Andrew, by the way,' he called after me, 'but you can call me Hashi.'

I glanced back over my shoulder. 'Moon,' I replied.

His smile broadened as he stood in the street watching me walk away. I turned from him, his face remaining in my mind's eye.

I felt stirred by the meeting in a way that had not occurred since first meeting you, my love. A sense of shame came upon me as a result. I thought of you, guilt making its presence known as I made my way back to our boy.

* * *

I stood in the street and watched her leave. The sight of her face had initially banished all words and left me speechless. Only once before had I been struck dumb by a woman's face. Only once before had my heart leapt at the sight of such striking eyes.

'Chula,' I said to myself, smile remaining and unable to tear my gaze from her diminishing form.

'Is everything all right, Andrew?'

I turned, finding Wilson standing nearby with his hand cart before him, the wide brim of his hat banding his eyes in shadow.

'Chula,' I repeated.

'What?' The white trader, who was a familiar face in the town, looked at me in puzzlement.

I shook my head in an attempt to bring order to my thoughts, to shake loose the impact of the chance meeting. 'Do you know anyone called Chula?'

Wilson thought for a moment, releasing the near handle of his cart and scratching his goatee. 'Can't say I have,' he replied with a shake of his head. 'Why do you ask?'

'Oh, no reason,' I responded. 'What are you selling today?'

'I've some furs and cotton blankets, and for my more discerning customers...' He reached forward and lifted the corner of the aforementioned blankets, revealing some glass jugs containing clear liquid. '...Moonshine,' he finished in a conspirational whisper. 'You want one?'

I shook my head, looking across the street at the saloon and wondering if Edwards would know of Chula. 'I'll be seeing you,' I stated, setting off towards the doors without hesitation.

Entering the saloon, I found it empty.

'We ain't open yet,' stated Edwards as he stood on one of the tables to take the glass covers from the candelabra above.

'I'm not after a drink, only information,' I responded.

He turned. 'Oh, it's you,' he said, rubbing his nose on his shirt sleeve in order to rid himself of an itch as he lifted the glass off. 'I told you yesterday, there ain't any work. Sugar-Plum deals with everything relating to back of house and me front of house,' stated the portly white man, referring to his wife, Sarah.

'I haven't come by to ask again,' I stated, the man not truly listening to me as he set the first glass cover by his feet on the tabletop and reached for the second. 'I just wondered if you know anything of a woman called Chula.'

'What?' he asked distractedly, taking it down and having to rub his nose again as he stifled a sneeze, the dust loosed by his activity irritating his large hairy nostrils.

'Chula, have you heard of her?'

'I ain't no information centre. Go ask at the administration offices,' he answered dismissively, placing the second shade by the first and then looking over his shoulder to check the location of the chair he'd used to climb up.

Frowning, I exited the dingy establishment where many of my peers spent a good deal of their time. I paused outside, a small flock of sheep being corralled along the street in front of me by a father and his young children. The former followed behind, a long stick in hand that was used to encourage the ewes at the rear to hurry along, his son and daughter to either side and struggling to keep the others from straying as bleats of alarm rang out along the street.

He looked over and nodded, touching the brim of his hat before taking the stick to the hind legs of one of the sheep, which leapt away and caused others to almost push the girl over. I nodded in return as I tried to think of anyone who might know something about the enigmatic young woman who'd had such an impact. I knew there were likely to be records of all those belonging to the Chickasaw Nation in the administration offices, but I also knew it was unlikely they'd let me see them.

'Bartholomew,' I stated to myself, thoughts turning to the old medicine man who was little more than a drunk and lived in a rundown shack on the edge of town, trading fortunes for drink.

Heading west, I followed the flock along the street, eager to pass, but seeing no way to do so. They veered off after the cattle pen on the right-hand side, taking the animals to the Wednesday market, pigs and other sheep already penned and awaiting auction, the air filled with their cries.

I saw Wilson with his cart talking to a couple of Chickasaw farmhands, a jug being taken from its concealment and changing hands after coins had been exchanged. I went over to him, glancing over the fence of the street-side pen to see a handful of piglets within, not long weaned.

'I've changed my mind,' I stated. 'How much for a jug?'

'Five pennies,' he replied, glancing at the administrative building, the authorities well aware that he was selling contraband and most of the settlement aware that he paid the law officers part of his profits in order to be overlooked.

I delved into the pocket of my brown britches. I had little coin left, my last work having been a week before. Pulling them out, I pushed them about on my palm with a fingertip. 'Will this do?' I asked, holding them out to him.

Wilson looked at them in contemplation for a moment. 'Seeing as you've been a steady customer in days past,' he said with a nod, referring to the months I'd spent inebriated after the death of my wife and child.

He took the payment and passed me a jug, my palms clammy as I took it and recalled those dark months of delirium and supposed escape. 'Much obliged,' I stated, setting off once again and trying to ignore the voice of the moonshine at my side.

* * *

I approached the Olsens' farm, walking across the grassland. Their dog was resting on the porch, her honey coloured fur giving rise to the Swedish name of Honung.

The beat of hooves drew my gaze to the right and I found Nicky riding towards me. Anders sat behind him, keeping him securely in place with his arms as they rode bareback. Confronted with our son's face, one which had inherited so much from you, the sense of guilt I'd previously felt was redoubled, unsettling me as I watched.

'Ishki!' called Nicky, nervously raising a hand from the mane of the deep brown mare and quickly taking hold once again as the beast began to gallop.

I raised my had in turn, smiling despite the guilt and the trepidation I felt at the sight, worried that he'd somehow fall despite the presence of Anders.

It thundered by, the thump of its hooves rising through my boots. Nicky laughed, the wind against his face and eyes narrowed.

Anders circled the horse, slowing its pace to a canter and then a trot. Coming back towards me, he brought the beast to a halt, its flanks dampened by perspiration as it tossed its head and snorted. Honung was making her way over from the house, having noticed my presence and tail wagging in response.

'Did you see, Ishki? Did you see?' asked our son excitedly.

'I saw,' I nodded.

'He'll be riding alone in no time,' commented Anders. 'A natural.'

Nicky beamed. 'You think?' he asked over his shoulder.

'It is clear to me. You have the posture and the confidence.'

'Can I ride alone?' He looked down at me hopefully.

'When Anders feels you are ready,' I answered, bending to fuss the hound as she sniffed the hem of the cloak.

'How long will that be?' He enquired, craning his neck to look at the Swede.

'Not long, I think,' he replied. 'You'd best get down and I'll be taking Rödbeta back to the stable,' he added, the horse having been named in Marie and Anders' native tongue for its favourite food; beetroot.

I put down the partially filled sack of corn, walking over and holding out my arms.

'I can get down by myself,' insisted Nicky, having inherited a strong sense of independence from me.

'I just thought you may like a helping hand.'

He was blushing slightly, feeling embarrassed by what he saw as babying, especially in front of Anders. 'I don't need your help.'

I stepped back and he awkwardly hooked one leg over Rödbeta's neck, sliding down her side and dropping to the ground. I noticed his bare feet and smiled as Honung went over to him.

'What?'

'You have taken off your boots.'

'It's easier to ride without them,' he said defensively, still a little perturbed by my motherly display.

'He insisted,' said Anders, thinking that maybe he wasn't supposed to remove them.

'It is fine,' I said, looking up at the Swede. 'I used to go barefoot all the time when I was a girl and do so on many occasions still, as I am sure you have noticed.'

'Indeed,' he responded with a nod. 'I will get Rödbeta to the stable and clean her down. Marie is in the house and expecting you, I think.'

'Thank you for taking him riding.'

'We can do the same tomorrow, if that is well with you.'

Nicky looked to me, apparently worried that I would refuse.

'That would be fine,' I replied.

Anders nudged the horse in the flanks. Turning her, he set off at a trot towards the house, the farm buildings and livestock to the rear. The fields had purposefully been located to either side, leaving grassland before the house and a clear view of the rolling hills beyond.

'Come on, let's go inside and see Marie,' I said, stepping away and picking up the sack. 'Maybe she will have made some of those honey and oat cakes you are so fond of.'

'You think?'

'We will have to see,' I responded as he ran to catch up and Honung trotted ahead of us.

I looked down at him. 'Anders is right, you know.'

'About what?' he enquired as he walked beside me.

'That you will make a fine rider.'

He grinned. 'I love the feeling of the wind on my face when she gallops and the thump of her hooves on the ground.'

We reached the house and stepped up to the porch, the door still open on the fine day. Nicky followed the hound inside, knocking and entering without waiting for a reply.

Following him in, I went to the table on the right and set down the sack. 'This is for you,' I said, Marie brushing the ash out of the fireplace on the other side of the room.

'Are you certain you're not in need of it?' she asked over her shoulder.

'I have plenty. Besides, you put it to better use. I don't know how you get your bread tasting so good, but it always outdoes mine.'

'Have you baked any of the oat cakes?' asked Nicky after scanning the kitchen area.

'I haven't, but if you would like some, I can do so when I'm finished with the fire.'

'If it's no trouble.'

'For you, never,' she responded, smiling warmly at our son.

I could see Marie's love for him in her expression, the sun slanting in and bathing her face in warmth. Golden flecks of dust moved lackadaisically before her eyes, as if the affection displayed in them were manifesting, were reaching out towards him.

I knew she was thinking of the lack in their lives, the longing clear in the way she gazed at Nicky. She did not speak of it often, but when she did it was obvious that she felt inadequate. She knew how much Anders wanted children, especially a son to carry on the name, and wanted more than anything to bear them, to give expression to their love in the continuation of their family.

'We could stay for the rest of the day, if you and Anders do not mind,' I suggested.

She turned to me and nodded. 'That would be a great pleasure,' she said, her smile tinged with sadness.

'Thank you,' she mouthed when Nicky's attention was taken by a bee buzzing about the door, aware that I had detected her wish for company.

* * *

I walked into the shack, the air thick with the mingling smells of mould, body odour and wood smoke. Bartholomew sat before the fire pit in the centre of the earthen floor, head bowed, hair ragged and hanging over his face. A moth-eaten sheepskin was draped about his shoulders as he stared at the flames as if in a trance, his eyes bloodshot.

'Bartholomew,' I greeted with a nod.

He didn't respond as the flames writhed, disturbed by my entrance and the reaching wind.

I seated myself on the earth opposite him, settling in the same cross-legged position and starting to feel myself sweat in the stagnant heat. A sense of entrapment came upon me in the humble dwelling, the slatted walls closing in as the fumes stung my eyes. There was no light allowed in, the single window shuttered, only narrow beams of sunlight piercing the haze from small knotholes in the front wall behind me.

I bent to look at his face, trying to attract his attention.

He blinked and slowly raised his head. His brow creased, recognising my face, but mind too addled to fit it to my name.

'My name's Andrew,' I stated.

Bartholomew nodded. 'Andrew,' he rasped, licking his lips and looking at the untidy furs laying about him. Seeing the neck of a bottle peaking from beneath one, he revealed it and unstopped the top.

He lifted it to his lips, closing his eyes and sticking out his tongue in expectation of satisfying his need. Barely a drop fell from the bottle and he lifted his lids to stare into its emptiness.

Throwing it aside in agitation, it rolled upon the furs and came to rest with a gentle bump against the base of the wall. 'You have any?'

I raised the jug into view.

His reddened eyes brightened and he reached across the fire with a withered hand, nails long and ingrained with dirt.

'Be careful,' I said, afraid the drooping sleeve of his dark shirt would catch alight.

'Give it to me.'

'I need information,' I stated, keeping it out of his grasp and watching the flames threaten to take to his arm.

He glared at me, brows tight and lowered. 'What information?' he asked, coughing briefly.

'Do you know of someone called Chula?'

He looked to the flames. 'Chula?' he asked them.

I wondered if he expected confirmation and started to think the visit was a waste of my time. I noticed that he was swaying back and forth slightly and realised he'd probably been drinking since waking. In his stupefied state, I felt it unlikely that he'd be of any assistance.

'Chula?' he asked again.

'Yes, Chula.'

He flashed me an annoyed glance before turning his attention back to the claws of heat within the pit. 'I have only known one with that name, but she is one that should not be spoken of.'

I looked at him in confusion. 'Why?'

'She was cast out of the Nation many years ago.'

'Cast out!' I exclaimed in surprise.

He lifted his head once again, regarding me closely. 'Where did you see her?'

'I never mentioned seeing her.'

'Why else would you be asking after her?' he countered.

I thought for a moment, detecting the seriousness of his enquiry. 'I saw her in the woods.'

'And yet she gave you her name.' He was clearly unconvinced.

'I hadn't seen her before and so asked after it,' I responded without pause. 'She told me as she walked away.'

'You are not to go near her.'

'Surely you can tell me why?' I pressed.

Bartholomew stared at the flames as if seeking permission from them to tell me the cause of her banishment. Nodding, he looked at me with utmost seriousness. 'She ran away with a nigger slave that her father had purchased.'

'That's Chula?' I said in surprise, recalling the story of the Chickasaw girl and the slave, the tale having been related to me in salacious whispers by tongues loosened by alcohol. 'They ran off together and her father tracked them down, shooting the nigger,' I stated. 'I hear she had a child by him after he was to the grave.'

'I hear it is so,' he confirmed.

'Where does she live?'

The old man's eyes narrowed and he took a deep breath as if fighting back nausea. 'Why would you want to know?' he asked, swallowing hard and perspiration starting to run down his forehead. 'She is no longer of the Nation and no one is to have anything to do with her.'

I tried to think of a valid reason, but came up with nothing but flimsy excuses. The flames drew my attention and I stared at their movements as I wondered at her location. The landscape of the Indian Territory was vast and the likelihood that I'd find her was slim.

An idea came to me and I looked up suddenly.

'What?' asked Bartholomew suspiciously.

'Thank you for your information,' I stated, ignoring his question and getting to my feet.

He coughed and spat up some phlegm, spitting it to the flames, which hissed in response. 'You're not to seek her out, you hear me?'

'I swear I'll do no such thing,' I stated.

The old man held my gaze and then held out his hand again. 'The jug.'

I looked down at the moonshine, having temporarily forgotten its presence. Holding it out to him, he snatched it from my grasp and opened it as quickly as he could, raising it to his lips.

Coughing and spluttering, he turned to the side and vomited on the furs, the stench of bile and alcohol mixing with the other odours within the shack. Wiping his mouth with the back of his free hand, he took a few breaths and raised the jug again.

I stepped to the rickety front door, glancing back to see him drinking it down as if it were water, my nostrils flaring. I vacated the shabby dwelling, gratefully inhaling the fresh air, though catching the scent of the shack upon my shirt as the breeze washed about me.

Walking away, I tried to recall as much of the story about Chula as I could, filled with excitement at the prospect of seeing her again.

* * *

Our son busied himself with eating the oat cakes that Marie had placed on a plate for him, blowing before taking each bite. Others cooled on a tray on the windowsill as Honung sat attentively watching Nicky in the vain hope of receiving a treat. Marie and I sat on two wooden lounging chairs that faced the window as Nicky perched at the table, licking the tip of his finger so as to collect up crumbs that had fallen to the plate.

'I wish he would eat my food with such eagerness,' I commented with a grin.

'You are a good cook,' she replied with a glance.

'If I make a meal and manage not to burn anything, I regard it as a success.'

Marie chuckled. 'I'm sure it isn't so,' she stated. 'I have tasted your food many times and have never had any complaints.'

'Just stomach pains,' I joked.

She laughed again. 'Anders is particularly fond of the meatloaf you make and has asked me many times to make the cornbread.'

'You do not have to be a good cook for either.'

'You do yourself injustice,' she said as we both watched a bird gliding high in the sky, its silhouette passing beyond the window frame and out of sight.

'Can I have some more?' asked Nicky, looking over after sucking the tips of his fingers to get the last residue of honeyed sweetness.

'No more food until lunch,' I stated before Marie could speak, knowing that she would never refuse him.

He frowned. 'Just one more?'

I shook my head. 'You should be grateful Marie made those.'

'I've already said thank you,' he protested.

'I'll wrap them and you can take them home with you,' she said, giving him a wink.

Nicky immediately brightened.

'What do you say?' I prompted.

'Thank you, Auntie Marie,' he grinned.

Anders swiped a cake as he passed outside the window. 'What are we having for lunch?' he asked through a mouthful as he stepped through the door, Honung glancing over, but remaining by Nicky's side with begging eyes.

'You're not to be eating anymore of the cakes. They're for Nicky.'

'All of them?' He looked at his wife in surprise as he loosened the faded red neckerchief he was wearing, his blonde hair unkempt as usual.

'All of them. I will send him home with them.'

'You're a lucky boy,' he said. 'When I was your age I would get a few salted fish if I was hungry between meals.'

'Salted fish?'

'We lived near a lake and my father would take the boat out. I'd go with him on days when I wasn't attending school,' expanded Anders as he bent and took off his boots after putting what remained of the cake into his mouth.

'There was forest all around and I often went exploring the rocky shore. To me the lake was like an ocean, the far shore beyond sight.'

'I am surprised you emigrated,' I said. 'Whenever you speak of it, it is with an air of nostalgia.'

Anders walked over to the kitchen table, briefly resting a hand on Nicky's hair as he passed and went to the pantry door. 'It was the winters that drove us to these shores,' he stated. 'I have spoken of it before.'

I nodded. 'They were long and dark,' I responded as he looked inside the small room.

'And there were often deep snows.' His voice had a hollow quality as it drifted from within the pantry, Anders leaning in to scan the foodstuffs.

'We have snow here.'

'Without the long dark and Arctic cold.'

'Dark enough,' I replied.

'Do we have bread and cheese?' he asked, looking around the frame at us.

'They're already on the table,' said Marie with amusement.

He straightened and looked over his shoulder, seeing the items already placed in the centre of the tabletop. 'I was preoccupied,' he responded, closing the door as Nicky chuckled.

'With the oat cakes and our honorary son.' She glanced at me surreptitiously, having never used the term within my hearing before.

Catching the look in the periphery of my vision, I turned to her questioningly. 'What?'

'Nothing,' she replied with over emphasis, quickly getting up from the chair.

She passed behind Nicky and went to the pantry, briefly disappearing from view before returning with the butter dish in hand. She placed it on the table and took off the lid. 'In case anyone does not want cheese,' she stated.

Anders stepped to her and slipped an arm about her waist, giving her a kiss on the cheek in belated greeting.

'What's Swedish for horse riding?' asked Nicky.

The Swede placed his free hand on Nicky's shoulder as our son looked up at the couple. 'Hästridning.'

'Hästridning,' repeated Nicky to himself. 'It's not that different.'

I looked at the three of them together on the other side of the room, Anders' hand upon Nicky's shoulder and his arm about his wife. The sight was disconcerting. They had the appearance of a family, the darker tones of our son's skin notwithstanding.

'Nicky,' I called, patting the seat of the chair nearby which had recently been vacated by Marie.

He looked over. 'We're just about to eat,' he responded, Anders' hand remaining upon his shoulder.

'Come sit at the table,' stated Marie, moving out of her husband's loose hold and taking the far seat.

Anders moved to the nearest, seating himself with his back to me as I rose to my feet. The Swedes flanking our son, I was left with only one option and took the chair opposite Nicky, my back to the open door and able to feel the warmth of the sun as its light streamed in.

'How many slices, Nicky?' asked Marie, the hound moving to sit nearby.

'Two, thank you,' he responded, having got into the habit of saying thank you rather than please after discovering the latter word didn't exist in the Swedish language.

She cut the slices and placed them on the top plate of a pile resting before her. 'Cheese or butter?'

'Cheese.'

She nodded and picked up the slicer. Drawing it across the top of the block of cheese, a thin slice was cut and gently laid on one of the rounds of bread. Repeating the process, she then handed him the basic lunch and focussed her attention on me. 'Chula?'

'The same will be fine,' I responded, still feeling unsettled. I can't deny that I felt a pang of jealousy as I thought about all the times Nicky visited without me. Were they like a family then? Did our son laugh and interact with them as he would me? Did he see Anders as his father?

'Here,' she said, holding out the plate to me.

'Thank you.' I set it before me, not truly having any appetite.

Waiting until she had served Anders and herself, I then sat with back straight and eyes open as they placed their hands together in readiness to give a prayer of thanks. The feelings that were already rife within me intensified when I noted our son following suit.

'Nicky,' I whispered, looking at him disapprovingly.

'He has taken to joining us in saying Grace,' said Marie. 'We didn't think it would do any harm.'

'Your beliefs are not his,' I stated sharply, my feelings given expression in my tone.

'They are yours,' said Anders pointedly and in defence of their actions.

'They are his peoples',' I countered, turning to him.

'You have said that God and the Great Spirit are just different names to explain the same thing,' said Marie.

I turned the other way, feeling caught between them. 'I have, but Great Spirit is the term he should use,' I responded, knowing that I was being both unfair and purposefully awkward.

I saw her look to Anders and glanced over my shoulder.

'Have we done something to upset you?' asked Marie softly, reaching out and setting her hand on mine.

I withdrew from the touch as if from a snake bite. She looked at me in confusion, staring into my eyes as if to seek out the reason for my behaviour.

'We are not Christ worshippers,' I stated, looking to the untouched food on my plate.

There was a temporary and uncomfortable silence.

I took a breath. 'I am sorry.' I looked up at her.

'We understand your visits to see your sister must be... How you call it? Stressful?'

'They are,' I responded.

'There is often a little agitation when you return,' commented Anders, 'though today it is worse than I have seen it before.'

'We did not have much time today,' I responded, using the excuse for my irritableness that they had presented me with, not wishing to reveal the jealousy I was feeling.

It was then, as I sat in sight of their sympathetic expressions, that I realised the meeting with the Chickasaw man had also brought tension. Two aspects within me were straining against each other, as if each pulled on the end of a rope and my tension arose from its tautness. My loyalty and love for you held one end while my undeniable attraction to the man tugged at the other. And in that latter admission I was awakened to something I had not encountered before; a yearning for companionship.

'It is a shame she can't come to you when her husband is at his work,' commented Marie.

'Pardon?' I asked, having been distracted.

'Your sister,' she said, 'it is a shame she cannot visit you.'

'A woman should not be encouraged to deceive her husband,' stated Anders, looking disapprovingly across at his wife.

'Should sisters be kept apart.'

'There is reason,' he said, not wishing to expand further for fear of offending me.

'Love was the reason.' I looked at him. 'The love between Nicholas and I was the reason I was cast out. Do you believe love to be a sin?'

Marie raised her eyebrows as she regarded her husband, challenging him to defy what I'd said.

'It is true,' he conceded after a moment. 'Love was part of the reason.'

'Part?' asked Marie.

'Let's not speak of this,' he said, glancing at me.

'You are right,' agreed Marie, nodding. 'Let us speak of good things.' She said with a forced smile. 'How are your crops coming?'

'The birds take their share, but the growth is good and there is still plenty,' I replied, happy not to delve into the past again, as we had on a number of occasions during the years of our friendship, usually resulting in the loss of my temper.

'Anders could make you a...' She looked to her husband. 'What is fågelskrämma in English?'

He pondered. 'Scarecrow?' he said, looking to me without certainty.

'Scarecrow,' I nodded. 'There is no need. The creatures are welcome to their share.'

'You don't mind?' asked Anders in surprise.

'You have had the same reaction before and I had the same answer. The land is not mine, but is shared with all life that seeks sustenance from it.'

'It is the same as when he didn't notice the bread and cheese upon the table,' smiled Marie. 'He hears and sees only what his mind is able.'

'I remember now,' he protested, leaning forward.

'And now you see the bread and cheese, but not that your neck tie trails on them,' said Marie, winking at Nicky.

Our son laughed as Anders looked down and pulled the red neckerchief from his food, leaning back as he did so. A slight flush to his cheeks, he picked a hair from one of the slices.

'There,' he began, 'they can still be eaten.'

'Then let us say Grace,' said Marie.

Nicky's smile faded and he looked across at me pleadingly.

I nodded begrudgingly, knowing that you would have allowed him to join them in offering up the prayer of thanks and imagining you watching over the scene.

He put his hands together and closed his eyes.

'For what we are about to receive, may the Lord make us truly thankful,' said Marie.

'Amen,' they all said in unison, the sound of Nicky ending the prayer with the Swedes making my heart ache.

I had thought he would continue with the traditions of the Nation, but he was slipping away from them like so many before. I accepted that his blood was not pure, that he shared a heritage with both the Chickasaw and the Africans that had been brought to these shores, but had not thought to find him adopting the beliefs of the white folk.

'Are you not hungry?' asked Marie.

'Not really, but I will not let the food go to waste,' I replied.

Folding one of the slices of bread over upon itself, I took it to my mouth. I ate slowly, forcing it down, but knowing it was needed in order to see me through the rest of the day.

'Can I have some more, thank you?' asked Nicky.

'Here,' I said, 'have my second piece of bread.' I slid my plate over to him.

He looked to Marie for permission to take it, the sight rankling me. I was his mother and it was from me he should have been seeking agreement.

She nodded and he picked it up, careful not to let the cheese slide from it. I tried to remain calm, telling myself that the bond our son had with the Swedes was harmless. They were good people with kind hearts. In the years that I had known them they had been reliable and consistent friends.

'Will you stay for the afternoon?' asked Anders. 'I will be tending the cattle and I know Nicky likes to help.'

'Can we stay, Ishki?' he asked through a mouthful of food.

I looked to him. 'I have already told Marie we will stay,' I stated, looking to his eyes and being reminded of you, my love.

'One of the cows is close to calving, so it may be you will be helping me with the birth,' said Anders after swallowing the last of his lunch.

Nicky looked at him excitedly. 'You think…' He coughed, the food catching at the back of his throat.

Marie leant over and patted him on the back as his eyes watered. 'You should be finishing your food before you speak.'

'Enough!' I snapped, abruptly getting to my feet and the legs of the chair scraping loudly on the floorboards.

Everyone looked at me in shock.

Immediately regretting my outburst and seeing that I had made the dog jump, I tried to calm myself. 'I have had enough food and will take my leave,' I stated.

'You're going?' asked Marie.

'Only to sit on the porch,' I replied, going to the door and feeling the sun upon my face.

'Would you like me to bring out a glass of milk?'

I glanced back at her. 'Thank you,' I nodded.

Stepping out, I went and sat down at the edge of the porch, feet amidst the long grasses and wildflowers before me. A bee busied itself about them and I watched its activity as it went from flower to flower, legs heavy with its gatherings.

Honung padded out, as if aware that I was flustered and unhappy. She lay to my left, resting her head on her legs as we both looked to the grassland. Reaching out, I scratched her behind the ears and she looked up at me with soulful eyes.

'I am fine,' I assured her, trying to smile, but finding myself unable.

Footsteps caused me to turn, Honung raising her head but soon settling back down. Marie approached with a glass filled halfway.

'Here,' she said holding it out to me.

'Thanks.' I took the glass and cradled it upon my lap.

'May I join you?'

I nodded, returning my gaze to the view, a strand of pines running away from the cottage on the right and vibrant with new growth. Marie seated herself on the opposite side of me from the hound, remaining silent awhile as she too savoured the expansive landscape laid out before us.

'Is there something wrong?' she asked quietly as the sound of Anders and Nicky rising from the chairs drifted out to us.

'It was a short visit today,' I replied simply, not wishing to converse in truth.

'How was Esther?'

'Well.'

She studied my profile, her examination clear at the edge of my gaze. 'There is something more,' she stated with certainty.

Anders' boots thudded on the porch and we both turned to see him step down with Nicky close on his heels. They passed before us and went around the side of the house, our son briefly raising a hand in parting as Honung got up and followed them.

'Could you ever love another?' I asked, turning to look into her eyes.

'While I'm married to Anders?' she asked, staring at me with curiosity, never having heard me talk in such a way before.

I shook my head. 'If he were to pass away, would you be able to love again or would it be a betrayal of what you have?'

'Eight years is long enough to mourn,' she stated.

'I do not ask for me,' I said quickly. 'It was just a thought.'

Marie placed her hand upon my shoulder. 'It would not be a betrayal. The love you felt for Nicholas can still live in your heart while you love another,' she said softly. 'From what you have told me of him, he would wish for you to find joy with another.'

'There is no other,' I said defensively, resisting the urge to stand so that our contact would be broken.

'It may be that it is time to find one.'

'I am an outcast,' I responded, turning my gaze to the vista once again. 'And I have a child.'

'A child without a father.'

'He has Anders,' I replied, feeling guilty that I was using the very thing that had rankled me to argue my position.

She took her hand from my shoulder and rested it upon her lap with the other, knitting her fingers together as I raised the glass and sipped the cool milk. 'A closed heart is a gift yet to be... What is the word? ...Unwrapped. To love and be loved is the greatest gift.'

'I love him still.'

'I know,' she said, 'but it is a memory you love.'

'Let us not talk about it anymore,' I responded, feeling the tension growing in my shoulders.

'As you wish,' replied Marie.

We sat side by side for a short while, the birdsong replacing our conversation as the sun slowly arced through the heavens.

'Shall we go and see if the birthing is taking place?' she asked. 'Maybe we can witness a new life coming into the world.'

I nodded, but said nothing.

Rising, Marie held her hand out to me. I took it and got to my feet. Keeping hold, she took me around the side of the house and we made our way to the pasture where the cattle grazed.

* * *

Anders and Nicky pulled, the strain clear on their faces. The calf remained in station, its front legs sticking out from the rear of the heifer, a rope tied about them as the men tried to deliver it into the sunshine.

The cow bellowed in distress as they pulled again. Still there was no sign of movement.

'Should we help?' called Marie as we stood by the fence and watched.

'One more try,' replied Anders. 'We must put all our strength into it,' he stated over his shoulder, Nicky nodding in response.

They pulled, the Swede gritting his teeth and knuckles white as he gripped the rope. With sudden release, the calf slid from its mother, glistening with moisture. Anders stumbled back, Nicky dropping to his rump.

Moving forward as the cow inspected its child, Anders undid the rope about the calf's legs and stepped away. Steam rose from the newborn as it lay upon the grass and we all waited to see signs of life.

It raised its head, which wobbled from side to side as the creature got used to the sudden weight of its own existence. It produced a small sound, more akin to the bleat of a goat than low of a cow. Its mother began to lick the afterbirth from its skin, nuzzling its head briefly as it continued to make its cry.

'She loves it,' stated Nicky as he remained seated on the grass near the cows.

'As any parent loves their child,' responded Anders.

'Male or female?' called Marie.

'Female.'

'For that I am thankful,' she said to me quietly, hands upon the top bar of the fence.

I looked at her questioningly.

'I do not like killing the young bulls. Both their distress and that of their mothers is hard to bear and I find myself having to go for long walks to try and cast their pleas from my mind.

'The first season we kept cattle, I was troubled by nightmares filled with their cries. I do not speak their language, but their anguish is clear.'

'But they provide you with meat for yourselves or to trade.'

Marie frowned and sighed. 'I would that we could survive without it.'

'Without beef?'

'Without any meat. Have you heard the cries of chickens when their necks are about to be wrung?'

I nodded, thinking on the occasions I had killed those that had stopped laying.

'We choose to ignore their pleas, but they beg us for mercy, for their lives.' She turned to me, the unmistakable sparkle of tears in her eyes. 'Life is a blessing, most of all to the creature living it. What right have we to take it?'

'It is the way of things.'

'And it is wrong,' she stated with absolute certainty.

'I didn't know you thought this way.'

'Anders does not like it. I think that deep within him, he knows the truth of it, but wishes not to accept it.'

'Look Ishki!'

I turned to our son and found him pointing excitedly at the calf. It had lifted itself on its front legs and was unsteadily trying to raise its hind quarters, not quite finding the strength to do so.

We all watched, its determination to rise and find its mother's milk finally bringing it to its feet. It moved to her udders, tottering slightly as it began to suckle and its mother licked along its flank.

'It is always a joy to see,' stated Marie, the glisten of sadness within her eyes replaced by one of gladness.

Anders walked over with the rope in hand. He looked to his wife, seeing the emotion of her gaze. He leant forward and they briefly kissed.

'She's a strong one,' he stated, turning to look back at the calf and her mother as Nicky approached. 'They usually take a little longer to get to their feet.'

'Did you see, Ishki? I helped with the birth,' said our son brightly.

'I saw and it was a great sight,' I smiled.

'Are there others that will be giving birth soon?' he asked, looking to Anders.

'There are two,' he confirmed with a nod, 'and if you're here, you can be helping with all of them.'

Nicky looked at me. 'Can I stay until all the calves have been delivered?'

'We will be coming by most days,' I responded, my smile fading. 'I am sure Uncle Anders and Auntie Marie do not want you under their feet all the time.'

'It is no bother,' said Marie. 'He can sleep in the spare room,' she added, the room once having been referred to as the barnkammare, which was Swedish for 'nursery' and had been dropped only recently. 'We will see he continues his reading when evening comes and Anders can help him do sums.'

'Can I?' Nicky looked up at me expectantly, his pleading and innocent gaze reminding me of the calf.

Fighting against the urge to refuse, knowing that I had no sound reason to do so, I finally nodded. 'Just until the calves are born.'

'Can we go riding every day?' he asked eagerly, turning to Anders.

'I'm sure I can find the time,' replied the Swede, 'but only if you help with Rödbeta's care.'

'I will,' he confirmed, an ear-to-ear grin upon his face that did nothing to ease my tension at the thought of leaving him at the farm.

I knew my feelings had no foundation, that our son loved me dearly and would never see others as his parents, but I felt time slipping away as he grew by the day. He was fast becoming a man and I would pass into memory upon my death, just as you have passed into memory, my love.

'I should go back and see to my chores,' I stated, looking to the Olsens and trying to smile.

Marie took my hand. 'We will watch over him and look to your return.'

'I will come by tomorrow,' I responded, slipping my hand from hers as I stepped away. 'Do as Uncle Anders and Auntie Marie tell you, and respect the world about you,' I said to Nicky in parting.

'I will, Ishki,' he replied with a nod.

I wanted to go to our son and take him into my arms, to hold and feel him close, but the fence barred my way. 'See you all tomorrow,' I said, turning and beginning the journey home.

* * *

I release the steer and it got to its feet with the brand still steaming on its rear. With a kick and buck, it set off to join the others gathered at the far end of the corral.

'How many's that?' I asked as Forrester put the branding iron back into the coals held in a brazier supported by three stout legs.

'Twenty Five,' he replied, the old Indian still fitter than many who were only half his age. His face was angular and weathered, eyes small but filled with the light of vitality.

'Ground the next,' he stated, adjusting his braces, the firmness of his chest clear beneath his deep blue shirt, the top buttons undone.

I nodded and moved towards the beasts. I looked at them, trying to identify those that remained unbranded. They nervously returned my gaze, bunched together and hooves lively upon the earth.

'It'll all be over soon,' I soothed, slowly approaching, ready to make a quick grab as I spied one of the few that had yet to receive its mark.

They began to break to the sides and I lunged, taking it about the neck with my arm. With a firm twist of its head, I forced it to the ground and placed my knee to its neck so that it reclined on its side.

Forrester took the iron from the coals and strode over, the young ox snorting and watching with trepidation, eyes wide. With quick firmness, he pressed the glowing S-shaped iron to its hind quarters. It gave a cry of pain as its flesh briefly hissed.

Removing the iron, Forrester inspected the brand and then nodded at me. 'You can release him,' he stated.

I let go, quickly stepping back as it got to its feet and rejoined the perceived safety of the herd.

'There's four more.'

I looked to him and wiped perspiration from my forehead with the back of my hand, glancing at the sun. 'Do you know anything of the outcast woman?' I asked, trying to blink the afterimage from my eyes, the red ball of the sun that was imprinted upon them temporarily obscuring Forrester's face.

'Abraham's daughter?'

'I think her name's Chula,' I said, trying to make my words seem like an innocent enquiry as I began towards the steers again, the continuing disturbance of my vision making it hard to distinguish which had yet to be branded.

'Ran off with a slave many years ago,' he stated flatly as he went to the brazier and pushed the iron into the coals, thin strands of smoke rising with the rippling heat. 'You shouldn't have anything to do with her.'

As I looked to the beasts ahead, it seemed to me that his final words were like the lowing of the cattle. The herd had turned their backs on Chula, but I wasn't one of them. I knew what it was to be on the periphery, to be shunned and looked down upon thanks to my time as a drunk.

'I hear she lives nearby,' I commented.

'The far side of Black Hill ain't nearby.'

I glanced back at him. 'Black Hill?'

'To the northwest. When the sun is in the west, the shadows of the trees on the nearside make it look black.' He looked beyond me. 'They're breaking.'

Turning forward, I found the herd splitting like water passing around a rock. Seeing one of the few still in need of Forrester's mark, I made a grab for it, but the beast escaped.

Forrester singled it out and took it down as it passed him. He got it onto its side with a look of determination. 'Andrew!' he called.

I ran to the brazier and took the branding iron out, moving to the steer with the smouldering end held high as I thought about Chula. There was a touch of nervousness in my stomach now that I knew her location, knew that I could find her and see her again.

I pressed the iron to the creature's flesh. It kicked with its hind legs and lowed in pain. Forrester looked to the mark and gave a nod of approval before releasing the ox.

I licked my lips as I watched the beast get to its feet, the call of the drink coming over me. The thought that it would settle my nerves, that it would give me courage to approach the woman that had set a fire in my spirit, caused me to think of the saloon and the temptation it offered.

'No,' I stated to myself forcefully, shaking my head. I had been without drink for over a month, though my reputation was still of a drunkard.

'No?' Forrester stepped over to me with a curious look and took the long handle of the iron from my grasp.

'Nothing,' I said, licking my lips again.

He looked into my eyes. 'The drink's calling you,' he stated.

'How do you know?'

'My brother,' he replied, walking back to the brazier.

I watched him, recalling how Daniel had been found dead by the stream that ran south of the settlement. People said he was sitting with his back to rocks near the shallows of Pike's Turn, a stupefied look on his face as he stared sightlessly across the rapid waters, an empty bottle of moonshine by his side.

'I didn't mean…'

'Don't give in to it,' he interrupted. 'He was free of the bottle for a time, but its call was too strong. You are better than that. Your spirit has great strength.'

Forrester held my gaze for a moment. 'Ground the next,' he instructed, turning to look at the coals and leaving me certain that the subject was thereby closed.

* * *

I arrived home and went straight to my room in order to change out of the dress I had worn to town. Glancing at Nicky's bed and hoping that he would sleep soundly at the Olsens' rather than wake with fearful screams, I went to stand at the foot of my cot.

Slipping the dress from my shoulders, I laid it upon the covers and picked up the buckskin britches beside. Bending to put them on, my gaze fell on the chest of drawers Anders had made for me and my brow furrowed. Positioned against the wall, the lower drawer was slightly open, but not from my hand as I hadn't had need to fetch out any linens for a good few days.

Pulling up the britches and putting on the traditional dress, I stepped to the drawers and crouched. Opening the bottom one fully, I peered inside to see if I could deduce if anything was missing.

My gaze settled on brown leather poking out from beneath the house linens collected within. 'The journal,' I whispered in realisation, only the tip of its upper corner visible and its presence having been all but forgotten.

I thought for a moment and glanced over my shoulder at Nicky's bed. 'It would explain his nightmares and their content,' I said to myself, sure that my assumption was correct and our son had been secreting the journal from its hiding place in order to read it.

Making a mental note to speak with him about it when I returned to the Olsens' the following day, I pushed the drawer fully in. Straightening, I glanced out of the window, able to make out the tops of the crosses that marked the graves of Coop's wife and child. Despite what he had done, I still maintained them. They were not responsible for his actions and I felt it my duty to respect their final resting places.

With a frown and a glance at the bottom drawer, I walked out of the room, remembering an occasion not more than three weeks previous when I had asked Nicky to fetch out a dish cloth. 'He must have discovered it then,' I stated, regretting not having hidden the journal better and saddened that he had read the terrible tale at such a young age. 'No wonder he has been having bad dreams.'

I walked along the short hallway and into the main room, my thoughts turning to you as I considered what was contained upon those pages. I had not read it since writing the last words, but had tucked it out of sight and mind. It had been by intention to read the journal with Nicky when he was older so that he would come to know more about you and the brief time we shared.

Going over to the far corner, I took up the broom and stared at the boards. 'I miss you, my love,' I sighed.

I stood in sad contemplation for a while as birdsong drifted in through the open door. With a scrape, I began to pass the switches over the floor, chasing the dust ahead of them and into the air, where it swirled in the light breeze as memories swirled in my mind.

* * *

The chores done, I stood in the doorway leaning against the post. The house had recently passed into the shadow of the hill behind and the temperature was dropping, gooseflesh rising on my bare arms.

I looked to the ruins of the barn, able to see it between the trees to the south. The thought of visiting your resting place came to mind and I stepped out to the path, my feet bare. Walking to the gate, I passed out and headed right.

Arriving at the entrance to the barn as it nestled in its scattering of trees, I hesitated and then entered. Going to the grave, I knelt beside and placed my hand upon the topmost stone. It still retained the heat of the sun, its gentle warmth upon my palm. I wished it were the warmth of your skin beneath my hand, my love. I wished I could feel your heartbeat.

'Our son is staying with the Olsens while the cattle give birth,' I stated. 'He helped bring a calf into the world today. You should have seen him. He sees the wonder in life.' My eyes sparkled with tears as I took a steadying breath.

'I have something to say to you, but I struggle to find the words,' I admitted. 'There was a man in the settlement. I was returning from Essy's when he stopped me in the street to warn that my grain was spilling.'

I took another breath, gripping the stone tighter as my body began to tremble with the force of my emotions. 'My heart was stirred by the meeting.' I bowed my head guiltily.

'I love you so.' I stared at the rocks, tears beginning to fall. 'What would you think of me?'

A flash of colour drew my gaze to the tumbledown gap in the wall opposite me. A robin sat on the stones, watching me with head slightly cocked to the side.

'Is that you, my love?' I whispered. 'Are you answering me?'

It hopped to the near edge, regarding me closely. With the brief flutter of wings, it moved to the high grasses in the lea of the wall, its red breast vibrant against the shadowed green of its surroundings.

I stared at it, blinking my vision clear. 'Nicholas,' I said softly, raising my hand from the rock and reaching out to it.

With a tweet, the bird took to the wing and flitted over the southern wall, disappearing from sight. I looked to gentle movement left in its wake and saw a single white feather floating before the stones of the wall, drifting to the grass.

The breeze reached in through the nearby doorway. The feather danced, moving further into the building and towards the grave, its pale form settling at the foot of the pile of stones.

I stared at it before rising to my feet. Stepping over, I took it from the grass and held it before me, watching the wind stroke the down with invisible fingers. A sad smile arose upon my lips as I lowered my hand and made my way out of the building.

I walked back to the house filled with a sense of calm after speaking to you and being visited by the robin. Reaching the gate and resting a hand on the top bar, I looked to the gloom visible through the doorway. Nicky's absence came to the fore. It had made itself known when I had sat at the table and eaten alone, deciding not to cook when there was only me to dine. Now, as night drew ever closer, the emptiness of the house was spoken of by the dark mouth ahead.

I removed my hand from the gate, deciding to walk some more in the hope that when I got back I would be weary enough to find sleep. I did not want to be awake and alone in the silence of the night.

I let my feet take me where they may, walking northeast across the vale into a strand of pines at the foot of the far hill. Their scent was heavy, the wind only a breath of passage that hadn't even the strength to stir the smallest of branches. Birds called as small moths were disturbed by my passing and flew between the trunks, finding rest in the ridged bark.

I paused and leant closer to one, careful to move slowly. Its pale wings were spread wide and decorated with patterns of black that camouflaged it against the trunk.

Blowing softly, it took flight and passed around the pine. I moved to the side to look beyond, but could see no sign of it.

I walked on, my feet sinking into the mat of needles and water seeping up about my toes, the earth made succulent by the spring rains. The feather was raised to my face as I passed out of the strand onto the slope of the eastern hill. I absently brushed it along my lips as I looked up, seeing the last sunlight upon the brow.

Climbing to the summit, I looked west. The last rays settled upon my face, the sun seeming as though it were setting against the brow of the hill opposite. I closed my eyes and breathed deep.

The tip of the feather was drawn across my eyelids as I gave thanks for my life, for our son, for my time with you and for the chance to experience the wonder and glory of the world. Somewhere in the vale a fox barked and I smiled, feeling the Great Spirit had replied.

Opening my eyes, I looked down upon the house, fields and trees. A thin mist was gathering in the vale, arising in the shadow of the western hill like the soul of the land.

Remaining to watch the last of the sun dip out of sight, I began the descent. As I neared the bottom of the slope my feet were kissed by dew and the chill in the air once more caused the skin of my arms to rise.

My pace increased and I made for the far side of the vale. Passing through the thickening mist, the shadows of trees drew into sight and then faded at my back as I turned south and made for the house. My feet became numbed and I hugged myself for warmth.

Arriving at the boundary fence to the north of the property, I went to the chicken coop and peered into the gloomy interior. I was able to discern some of the birds roosting on two lengths of timber that ran the width of the small building and guessed the others to be in the nesting box positioned by the back wall. Deciding to check their food and water in the morning, I closed the door.

I climbed over the fence and glanced at the graves of Coop's family to the right, the crosses indistinct in the paleness. Walking along the side of the house, I reached the corner and came to an abrupt halt, my heart suddenly tumultuous.

Standing on the other side of the gate was the figure I had seen the previous evening, stooped and robed in mist and shadow. It was looking in my direction, its face concealed by the conditions and a curtain of lank hair, though something in the vagueries of its features struck a cord of recognition.

'Inki?' I enquired tentatively.

No answer was forthcoming and I could not be sure of its identity.

'Is it you?' I took a tentative step closer.

The figure turned and walked south without a word.

I watched, kept in place by shock and uncertainty. It diminished, the mist drawing it into its arms until it was but a vague darkness and then nothing at all.

* * *

I toyed with the coins in the pocket of my britches, payment for helping Forrester with the branding. They chinked and in the sound was the temptation, the call. It was aided and abetted by thoughts of coming face to face with Chula again. Such wonderings set a tremor in me, one born mainly of fear. It had many faces; fear of finding her less than I took her to be upon our first meeting, fear of rejection, fear of loss should we come to more in time.

Then there was the guilt. My wife, Jane, had been my strength and my light. We had named our daughter Oka, meaning 'water,' deciding to give no Christian name, but to remain true to the heritage of our people. My feelings for Chula were so unexpected and felt like an invasion of the sacred space within my heart. It was a space that Jane and Oka had occupied for so long and which was still swollen with sorrow after their passing.

The drink continued to call as my fingers churned the monies. I saw Oka's pale face. She had succumbed to the whooping cough and lay still amidst the furs of our bed. Not yet in her fourth year, the white doctor had been unable to do anything more than prepare us for her death. She was at peace, but we were in torment.

Jane never recovered. Grief overtook her, consumed her. Then came the evening when I returned from the fields and found her in the pine wood behind the house.

Trying to shake the image of her hanging amidst the trees, I made for the saloon with pace quickening.

I passed out of the alley and onto the main street through the settlement. Setting my sights on the doors to the establishment, I went quickly to them.

Entering, Edwards looked over from behind the bar, Sugar-Plum leaning on it from the other side, the husband and wife having been in conference before my arrival. There was a scattering of customers, a few nodding their greetings to me and one slumped in the near corner, stupefied and snoring.

I strode to the bar and put my coins down. 'Whisky,' I said hoarsely as Edwards moved over to me.

'About time you had a drink,' said Sugar-Plum, her lips with a natural pout and painted bright red. Her cheeks were dusted and blushed with makeup which was gathered thickly in the wrinkles about her eyes. With an almost skeletal face, it made her look as if she were sickening and trying to cover up the fact.

I nodded in response as her husband took a bottle from the shelves behind him and unscrewed the lid, a glass already placed before me.

'Andrew.'

I turned to find Obadiah staggering towards me with a grin on his face, drool snaking down his chin. 'Can you spare one for me?'

I glanced at Edwards, finding him regarding the drunk sourly as I gave a nod of consent.

'Last of the big spenders,' scoffed Sugar-Plum, sniggering briefly, her bright pink dress contrasting with the drab surroundings and loose at the shoulders, their blades shadowed by hollows.

Obadiah bumped into me, using the bar to prop himself up. Seeing the second glass being placed on the bar, he slapped me on the back with the exaggerated force of inebriation. 'You're a good man,' he said, breath stinking and teeth missing or rotting. 'Unlike Stanley, there,' he added, looking to the barkeep briefly.

'If you ain't got money, you ain't getting no drink,' said Edwards.

'Won't let me have anything on my ticket and I haven't anything else,' said Obadiah, looking down at himself and tugging at the front of his pale shirt, which was stained with dirt and sweat, the stench of his body thick about him.

'Your ration ticket ain't no good here,' stated Edwards as he put the lid on the bottle and went back to talk with his wife, putting the whisky back in place as he did so.

'You and me,' said Obadiah, putting his arm about my shoulders as he took hold of his drink. 'We should get a bottle and go someplace friendly. What do you say?' He downed the alcohol in one and banged the empty glass on the bar.

'Hey!' warned Edwards with a glare.

'Come on, let's get out of here.'

'I'm fine,' I said, my elbows on the bar and face averted as I tried to breathe through my nose.

'You've got the money for it,' he said, reaching for the coins still resting before me.

I slapped his hand away.

Obadiah looked at me incredulously, taking an unsteady step backwards. 'Did you just hit me?'

'It's my money and hard earned.'

'Are you calling me a thief?' he asked with a scowl.

I shook my head, his appearance reminding me of how low I'd sunk in the wake of my loss; a ship at the bottom of an ocean of sorrow, but one that had escaped its heavy depths and Chula the new breath of wind in my sails. 'Here,' I said, pushing the other whisky towards him.

His gaze settled on the drink. 'That's more like it,' he stated, his expression immediately brightening as he reached for it, swaying and in need of the bar's support.

Leaving payment for the drinks, I quickly gathered up the rest of the coins and put them in my pocket. I began towards the door, but Obadiah's expression became pinched with confusion and he placed his spare hand to my chest to stop my departure.

'Where you going?'

'Home.'

He glanced at the coins as he tried to fathom my actions, looking utterly bewildered and with mouth hanging open. 'You're not buying a bottle?'

'No,' I said, shaking my head.

'What about another drink for me?'

I shook my head again, stepping to the side to avoid the detention of his hand and quickly walking towards the door so that he had no chance of catching up with me in his state of drunkenness.

'You ain't the man you used to be,' called Sugar-Plum, her words meant to mock me.

I paused in the doorway. 'And for that I'm glad,' I said over my shoulder before stepping out.

Lamplight shining from a few windows provided the only illumination as I went along the street, making for my brother's farmstead, which was located southeast of the settlement. I could still hear the call of the drink and its temptation set greater haste in my steps, wishing to be away from the town and any chance of succumbing.

* * *

I could not sleep. The sight of the figure at the gate had unsettled me and the possibility that it had been Inki brought memories of the past to the forefront of my mind, along with questions as to his presence. Every time I closed my eyes, I was presented with the image of your face after he had shot you. Such pain, such loss.

Rising, I went to the main room and lit a lamp before seating myself at the table. The emptiness of the house consumed me and within its belly I was small and vulnerable.

I looked to the shutters, thinking with a shudder that the figure could be outside. I imagined its dark and hunched form standing before the door, still and brooding. My discomfort grew as I listened intently, seeking evidence to support the disturbing thoughts.

The timbers of the house groaned and the hairs on the nape of my neck tingled in response. I looked to the gap beneath the door, the darkness seeping in filled with possibility. I saw it taking form, growing before me and coalescing into my father.

The idea came to me that he had died and had come to see me one last time, but it was quickly dismissed. I had seen Esther that day and she would have told me if he had passed to the hunting grounds of the ancestors.

'Maybe she did not know,' I whispered to myself, my voice doing nothing to alleviate the tension of the night, but instead adding to it as I thought of him listening outside.

'He cannot be outside if he is dead,' I said, trying to add volume to my voice, to find my courage and dispel the fear.

The barking of a fox gave me a start and I stared at the door with wide eyes.

Noting the shivering that was taking hold as I sat in nothing but my white nightgown, I decided to make a fire, hopeful that its heat and crackle would bring comfort. I got up, trying not to make too much noise as I took up the lamp and padded over to the hearth on the far side of the room.

Preparing it, I took a match from the mantle above. It was struck on the boards and put to the kindling, which quickly took. Seating myself on the edge of the nearest chair, I watched the flames grow, regularly glancing at the front door and the entrance to the short hallway. The feeling of something lurking beyond my sight filled me with agitation.

'If it had been Inki at the gate,' I began, trying to calm myself with the sound of my own voice, 'what other than death could have compelled him to come?'

It had been he who had proclaimed me cast out of the Nation and taken your life. I could think of no reason he would visit bar the realisation upon his demise that he had wronged me.

I shook my head. 'Ishki never came to me, and our bond was greater by far,' I stated to the flames, feeling the warmth growing against my skin. 'Neither did you, my love.'

The firelight danced in my eyes, reflecting the activity of my mind. 'The figure was seen yesterday as well,' I reminded myself. 'Which means it is likely not a ghostly visitation, but someone of flesh and blood.'

I tried to picture the face behind the curtain of hair in order to confirm its identity. There was the hint of features, but nothing definitive. I could not be sure it was Inki, especially after the years that had passed since our paths had last crossed.

I frowned as I reached for more wood and stoked the fire, finding it the only comfort. The sound of scraping on the roof caused me to look up to the eaves, my pulse increasing.

An owl hooted above. I let out a breath of relief as my attention returned to the flames and my mind churned with thoughts and questions.

* * *

I walked into the house to find my brother seated on a stool before the stove, its door open and the fire within casting a haunting light upon his face. He had already turned to my entry, an old buffalo hide about his shoulders as he looked to my face, searching for signs of drunkenness.

Delving into my pocket as I went over to join him, I held out my palm with the remaining pay resting upon it. 'Towards my keep,' I stated.

He looked to the money and then to my face once again. 'You haven't been drinking?'

I shook my head. 'Take it.'

He reached out from beneath the skin and took the coins from my hand. 'What work did you find?'

'Branding with Forrester,' I replied as I seated myself on one of the other stools and held my hands out to the heat issuing from within the stove.

I could feel his gaze still resting upon me, knowing that he still sought signs or scent of drink.

'You didn't visit the saloon or one of those you used to drink with?'

I frowned and turned to him, both of us sharing a similar appearance inherited from our father, but his eyes smaller and long hair woven in a plait that hung down his back. 'I went to the saloon,' I confirmed. 'Edwards poured me a whisky, but I swear I didn't drink it, Brother.'

He held my gaze and then nodded. 'I am glad. How was Forrester?'

'As sprightly as always. He seems to become sturdier with age and will probably outlive us all.'

Duncan smiled and gave a snort of amusement. 'I wouldn't be surprised at all. I remember how he outlasted us all during last year's harvest, even on the hottest of days.'

We both looked to the stove, my brother taking a log from beside and tossing it through the doorway. He leant forward, elbows upon his knees and expression becoming thoughtful.

'Emily was convinced you'd return as you once had and I'm glad you proved her wrong,' he admitted without taking his eyes from the flames.

'She wasn't far from being right,' I stated. 'The call was strong.'

'What caused you not to listen?'

'Obadiah. He was sight enough.'

'Yet you brought him to our house on more than one occasion after you abandoned your land.'

I recalled the times we'd blundered drunkenly through the door, waking my brother's children and causing Emily to fret. Duncan's anger had been great, but I had been too altered to care, too persecuted by my loss to give anyone else a thought. 'I am sorry, Brother. For a time, I was lost to myself.'

'May such a time never return.' He paused in contemplation. 'Have you thought about returning?'

'To my land?'

He nodded, face to the flames and hands clasped together as he continued to rest his elbows on his knees. 'It's not too late to be planting crops.'

'I can't,' I stated.

He turned to me. 'Surely enough time has passed.'

'I just can't.'

'You cannot stay here forever.'

I looked to him. 'You're throwing me out?'

Duncan shook his head. 'Emily is pregnant.'

I looked at him as his words sank in. The house was cramped, my brother already having fathered four children, with a fifth, there would be no space for me to remain. 'When is she due?'

69

'The doctor thinks another seven months as yet.'

'Congratulations,' I said flatly, turning to the stove.

'Return to your land, Brother. Return and find yourself a new wife. You are young and healthy.'

I said nothing in response as I considered telling him about Chula. 'You remember the story about the outcast and the slave?'

I saw him nod in the periphery of my vision.

'I met her.'

He stared at me until realisation dawned. 'You cannot consider such a thing. You will be banished from the Nation with her.'

'Most of the Nation has long turned its back on our traditions, taking instead those of the whites, even their religion. Why should she still be deemed an outcast?'

'She broke with our laws.'

'We have broken with our heritage,' I countered. 'Why should it be that she is any worse, that she is to be ostracised?'

'She committed an outrage against our people,' he stated firmly.

'She did no such thing, Brother,' I said, glancing at him. 'She fell in love.'

Duncan was silent a moment. 'Cast her from your mind. There are plenty of others from which you can choose a wife.'

'There are no others that I would have.'

'How many times have you met her?'

'Once.'

'Did you speak with her?'

'Briefly.'

'Then you don't know her. You only see what you want to see; an enigma.'

'An enigma of such beauty as to strike to the very heart of me.'

'And what of her heart? It's clearly poorly aligned. She fell in love with a black slave.'

'She holds our heritage dear,' I stated.

'You can know this from a brief meeting? How?'

'She uses no Christian name, but a Chickasaw one.'

Duncan shook his head in dismay. 'That does not mean she holds to the old ways.'

'She knew the meaning of my true name.'

'As would many on the reservation. You're projecting what you hope to find and nothing more.'

'No, it's more.'

'You cannot be certain, Brother,' he insisted.

I remained silent, knowing that his last statement was true and that there was only one way to gain that certainty; I would have to seek her out.

'Leave her be,' he said, as if reading my thoughts. 'There are others that still hold to the old ways, if that's what you look for.'

I nodded, but made no comment.

The touch of his hand drew my gaze as he rested it on my forearm.

'Please, Brother, do as I say,' he stated when I turned to him. 'No good can come of such a bond. Let her go as you have let go the drink, for she will bring you low, just as the whisky did.'

I gave no answer bar another nod. I would not put agreement into voice because I knew it would be a lie. My mind was set. I'd find the woman who'd so stricken me and discover if my heart would continue to sing her name.

Thursday, April 10, 1873

I woke in the chair before the fire, my lids lifting slowly. I was shivering, the cold wind causing the door to knock against its fastening and moaning about the window.

'Seems as though Anders may have been right,' I mumbled to myself, getting up and stepping to the shutters.

Opening them, I looked out at the vale, which was warped by the variations in the glass. The clouds were thick and low, moving down the valley from the north with haste. The trees on the far side were alive with movement and I searched beneath for any sign of the figure, seeing nothing untoward.

I yawned as I returned to the hearth and took up the poker leaning against the chimneybreast. Prodding the remains, I found that a few embers still glowed and proceeded to get the fire going.

Once the flames were established, I pulled the chair closer and seated myself, waiting impatiently to feel the warmth. Another yawn took me and a tear rolled down my cheek. Wiping it away, I wondered how much sleep I had managed to find. It felt like little, my eyes heavy with tiredness and body lacking energy.

Holding my hands out to the flames, I continued to tremble with the cold which had bitten deep. I could barely feel the heat through the numbness of my fingers, rubbing them together in an attempt to regain sensation.

Waiting a little longer and feeling as if the cold had settled in my bones, I rose and went to my room to dress. Wearing leather britches beneath my buckskin dress and taking down my cloak of furs from where it hung upon a nail by the bedroom door, I went back to the main room and sought out the heat of the fire once again. The lack of sleep helped keep my thoughts subdued as I stared at the flames, the chill within me slowly receding as I was restored to life.

Glancing over my shoulder, I looked to the stove and considered what to have for breakfast. I had no appetite and decided to go without until visiting the Olsens for lunch. Instead, I remained in place, not wishing to leave the fireside, the need to see to my chores and make my daily pilgrimage to your side building with every moment.

I looked to the sprigs of bunched sage hanging on the wall at the back of the room beyond the table. It had become a habit to walk through the house with a smouldering brand of the herb, its smoke intended to cast out any darkness and purify. Whenever Nicky or I had bad dreams, whenever we felt sadness or were unsettled, I would make my rounds.

I got to my feet and walked over, taking down the bunch furthest to the right. Lighting it at the fire, I blew out the flames and faced the interior. Wafting the smoke with my free hand, the scent caught in my nostrils as I began to pass through the room and a haze gathered in the air as I chanted softly.

I walked slowly along the corridor to my room. Moving to its centre, I continued to disperse the fumes before passing across the hall into Nicky's room.

Finally returning to the main room, I walked about the kitchen table and went back to the fire. Satisfied that the ritual had been done and that all darkness had been dispelled, I dropped the sage into the hearth and it was consumed in the brightening of the flames.

I stood a moment before walking to the window again. I stared out at the gate, the image of the figure standing beyond superimposed over the scene. Going to the door, I opened it and stepped out. Closing it before hastening along the path, I pulled the fur tighter about my shoulders as the wind tugged at it.

Looking to the ground on the other side of the gate, I saw the indents that showed the figure's presence not to have been that of a spirit or a figment of my imagination. In the watches of the night, I had thought that maybe I had been mistaken, but the evidence was clear.

I went back to the house with a frown, glancing south. The mist that had gathered at nightfall had been blown away by the strengthening wind and the view was clear. There was no sign of anyone watching, though there were plenty of trees scattered about the vale which offered concealment.

My steps faltered as my gaze settled at last on the barn and I came to a stop on the path. I had no will or urge to visit with you, the words I had shared at your graveside the previous evening still fresh and the feather that had been gifted resting on the table.

'Chi-hollo-li.' I gave my usual greeting to you and stared at the ruins, sadness arising in response.

Standing awhile, not wishing to carry the sorrow into the house after only just cleansing it of such feelings, I contemplated our son. I had need to speak with him in privacy about the journal, but also hoped I would witness him ride that day. The joy it gave him was plain to see and, in turn, it gave me joy to see him so thrilled.

I took a deep breath and continued into the house, gratefully shutting the door on the wind. Feeling its draught upon my bare feet, I stepped to the table and looked to its top through the thin haze of sage smoke, discovering that the feather was no longer present.

Crouching, I scanned the floor, but could see no sign of it, my brow furrowing. I glanced about the room as I remained on my haunches, narrowing my eyes as I looked to the shadows in the corners and still found no hint of its downy paleness.

'The wind,' I stated to myself, thinking that the disturbance of my exit and entry had likely sent the feather fluttering out of sight behind a piece of furniture or into a web in the eaves.

Staring upward as I straightened, I saw nothing but the roof beams and the underside of the slats. Saddened by the loss, I sighed and felt a touch of guilt. The feather had been a gift and I had failed to keep it safe.

* * *

'Has Duncan told you our news?' asked Emily after handing me a bowl of steaming oatmeal, placing a hand to her stomach as she stood beside me in a pale blue housedress, dark hair framing her rounded face and her kindly eyes marked by soft wrinkles.

'Yes,' I replied, looking up at her. 'Congratulations,' I added.

'That's my place,' complained Simon, the only boy that my brother had been blessed with, five years old and petulant.

Emily turned as he lashed out at Celia, who had seated herself next to her father, all of us on stools arranged before the stove. 'No hitting,' she snapped, walking over and grabbing his wrist as he made to strike his younger sister again. 'Duncan?' she said to my brother, who was closest to the warmth spilling from the open door.

He looked up, pausing in his task of feeding the youngest, Elsa, who had yet to reach two. 'We've spoken about this before, Simon,' he scolded.

The boy frowned as his mother released him. 'But that was my seat.'

'If you don't take another, you'll be going without your food,' threatened Emily as Duncan took up a spoonful and blew on it before feeding it to Elsa.

'Sit next to Uncle Andrew,' suggested Helena, the eldest at six years of age but with a much older head on her shoulders. She had an unusually stern and straight-backed appearance for one so young, reminding me of a school mistress.

I glanced at the empty stool to my right, knowing the children were a little wary of me despite not having recently exhibited any of the aberrant behaviour that had been induced by my depression and drinking. Simon looked at the seat and then to me, his expression showing his displeasure.

He stepped over and sat heavily, resting his bowl upon his knees. 'The food's gone cold,' he moaned.

'I can still see steam,' I stated.

He ignored me. 'I don't want it.'

'Then don't have it,' responded Emily as she took the last seat between the girls, something that Simon had been unwilling to do, their relationship consistently adversarial.

The boy hung his head.

'You can have mine if you like,' I stated, holding it towards him. 'It's still hot.'

Simon shook his head.

'No good will come of going without. If I don't eat in the morning, my stomach growls like a bear before too long and scares the cattle.'

'Really?' asked Celia, who was a pale and sickly girl.

I looked across at her. 'It's been known,' I nodded.

'Are you sure?' Helena regarded me doubtfully.

I winked at her, but her expression remained stern.

'I thought not,' she stated as her attention returned to the oatmeal upon her lap.

'Go on,' I encouraged, nudging Simon gently and handing my bowl over.

He took it and I picked up the one upon his lap. I began to eat, warmth still residing beneath the cooled surface of the boy's food. The scrape of spoons against bowls and the occasional cough filled the room, Celia struggling to shake the cold which had lingered a good few weeks and had taken her fearfully close to death, her cheeks still hollow and shadows beneath her eyes.

'Have you got any work today?' asked Duncan glancing over as he wiped away a spill from Elsa's chin with his thumb.

I shook my head as I swallowed. 'I will go to the Exchange when I've eaten and see if there is any work going.'

'It would be nice if you could get something regular,' said Emily.

'I worked for Forrester yesterday and he mentioned some fencing that will be needed soon.'

'He gave us his pay for his keep,' said Duncan, Emily looking to my brother with mild surprise.

'Thank you,' she said, turning back to me. Her response held more than just gratitude, it also contained her pleasure and growing esteem at discovering I had not used my wages to drink.

I nodded, knowing that my stay had cost them far more and that I would be in their debt for a long time to come. My brother did not see it in such a light, but Emily was of a different mind and I hoped to pay back what she felt was due.

'Can I go play on the swing?' asked Celia as she finished the last of her meal.

'It's too cold and there isn't much time until school,' stated her mother.

'I can wear another fur,' she replied, one already wrapped about her.

'You're still too frail,' interjected Helena.

'And you're not my mother,' countered Celia.

'No bickering,' chided Duncan as he began to eat the last of Elsa's food, the youngster refusing any more.

Celia stuck her tongue out at her older sister.

'Mother…,' began Helena.

'No I didn't,' defended Celia before the accusation could be made.

'What did your father just say?' asked Emily rhetorically. 'Either sit quietly or go and get ready for school.'

Celia glared at Helena as their mother sat between. Helena ignored her, raising her nose in the air as if above such petty displays. She got to her feet and stepped to the stove, placing her bowl on top.

'I'll go and get ready,' she stated. 'There is a spelling test today and I should practice some words.'

'Let's hope you come top of the class again,' said Duncan.

'Top of the class,' mumbled Celia, rolling her eyes.

'You could learn a thing or two from your sister's diligence,' stated Emily.

Helena grinned with self-satisfaction as she passed out of the room.

I put down my spoon and unintentionally released a small burp. Simon looked up at me, a smile finally dawning.

'I should go to the Exchange before anymore of the day is done,' I said, rising and reaching over to place my bowl atop Helena's. 'Thanks for the food.'

'I hope there's work for you today,' responded Emily.

'If not, I could do with some help seeing to the weeds in the back pasture,' stated Duncan as Elsa wriggled in his grasp, wanting to get down from his lap.

'I'll return before noon if there's no work,' I replied as he let the girl slip from his lap, Elsa taking an unsteady step to her mother and looking up pleadingly.

Walking to the front door as Emily passed her bowl to my brother and lifted Elsa onto her lap, I glanced back and felt a pang of sadness. The girl clung to her mother lovingly as Duncan got to his feet and ruffled his son's hair, smiling down at him as he passed.

Feeling the loss of Jane and Oka keenly, I donned my coat and hat before stepping out into the cold day. The wind caused me to lift the collar about my neck as I looked out over the fenced fields of my brother's land and began along the track that would take me northwest to the settlement, my shoulders hunched against the chill that was as much within me as without.

* * *

The Exchange came into view along the main street. It was a large building where the bi-monthly rations were given out and it had become the gathering place for those looking for work. A bench had been placed against the wall and there were already a few seated on its length, hunkered within their clothes and coats pulled tight. A couple of them had been drinking companions in my darker days, taking temporary labour to keep their addiction fed.

I approached and received a few nods of greeting. Perching on the near end, well away from the drunks that sat huddled and wraithlike, I buried my hands deep into my pockets.

Some days there was no work, those that had waited slowly dispersing in silence. With the spring having come, there had been more to do and I'd found myself being chosen more often than not as my reputation as an unreliable drunkard faded from the memory of my people.

Thompson, the Agent overseeing the town and local district of the reservation, came out of the administration building a little way down the street. His hat threatened to be loosed by the wind and he raised a hand, holding it place as he began towards us with one of the law officers trailing behind.

Coming to a stop before the bench after moving aside as a wagon passed, he cleared his throat as he continued to cling on to his stiff hat. 'The delivery of rations is expected today and we need four men to help with the unloading,' he announced.

He pointed at a man halfway along the bench whose name was Mark. 'You.'

Pointing at two other men in close succession, the three who had been chosen got to their feet and stepped away from the bench as Thompson scanned those remaining.

The officer stepped forward and whispered something in his ear as he was about to point at John Sebastian, who was one of the drunks with whom I'd once shared my misery. Changing his mind on the word of the officer, Thompson looked at those still seated and then pointed at me.

'And you,' he stated.

I got to my feet and joined the other men in the street. Those still seated watched with downcast expressions as the wind rifled their clothes and messed their hair.

'Follow me,' stated the Agent, making for the door to the Exchange near the end of the bench where I'd been seated.

We followed him, the officer to the rear as Thompson unlocked the door and we trailed into the building. The moan of the wind echoed about its vacancy, most of the shelving lining the walls and regimented upon the dusty floor being empty.

'Get the loading bay open and give the place a clean,' instructed the Agent, looking about the interior.

We glanced at each other questioningly, wondering who should open the large double doors. Breaking from the rest, I strode towards them and lifted the wooden bar that kept them sealed. The wind immediately pushed them open to reveal the street and wide yard at the side of the building. Seeing a rock to either side, I used them to secure the doors against the walls, having seen them used for the same purpose when collecting my rations.

Turning, I discovered the building to be filled with swirling dust. Narrowing my eyes and breathing through my nose, I stepped to where a couple of brooms were leant against the wall beside a small window that looked out onto the street.

'There's no point with the wind as it is,' stated Mark as I began to sweep.

'Are you prepared to work or not?' asked Thompson, staring at him unkindly as he covered the lower portion of his face with his hand and stifled a sneeze. 'Get to the sweeping and you two start cleaning down the shelves,' he ordered, looking to the remaining pair as Mark reluctantly moved to take the other brush.

* * *

There was no sign of our son as I approached the Olsens' farm, though I had hoped to see him after spending the early part of the morning seeing to the chickens and household chores. Neither could I see Anders or Marie as I followed the vague trail across the grassland, the wind against my face causing me to narrow my eyes. I listened for any hint of his whereabouts, but could hear nothing above the whispering grasses and rush of air against my ears.

It was still only mid-morning and I thought it likely they were seeing to chores, Marie within the house while Anders and Nicky tended the livestock to the rear. My mind brought forth thoughts of accident and injury. I cast them aside, knowing that such projections were of little help other then in distracting me from what was evident.

I reached the house and stepped onto the porch. Knocking, I entered and shut the door behind, looking about the main room. 'Marie?'

There was no reply.

'Marie?' I called again with greater volume.

Moving to the rear of the room, I listened at the entrance to the hallway, hearing the shutters in the bedrooms rattling in place, such was the power of the draughts passing about the windows. I frowned and turned back to the door.

It opened unexpectedly, giving me a start. Marie entered and closed it, not seeing me until she faced the interior.

She let out a shrill yelp of fright. 'You scared me,' she said breathlessly, placing a hand to her chest. 'I didn't expect to find you here so early in the day.'

'Sorry,' I replied. 'I did not think you would mind.'

'I don't,' she said, moving around the table to the pantry. 'I was about to start preparing lunch. I thought something warming would be good on such a day as this.'

'Where is Nicky?'

'Another calf has been born. He is with Anders taking it and the mother into the barn. They have already taken yesterday's newborn there to shelter from the weather.' She ducked into the pantry. 'What do you think I should make?' Her voice issued out of the doorway to the small room.

'Broth?' I said without conviction.

'Yes, broth. That is a good suggestion.'

She soon reappeared carrying an assortment of vegetables, a couple of large squashes dominating. 'We can chop these and add some rabbit meat.' She placed them on the tabletop. A potato rolled away and she caught it just as it was about to fall over the edge.

'Is something wrong?' she asked.

'I was just a little startled by your entry,' I replied, 'as you were by finding me inside.'

'We gave each other a fright,' she smiled warmly. 'Do you mind seeing to the rabbit?' she asked, not relishing the task and Anders usually attending to the meat that was to be included in any meals.

'Not at all,' I replied as I stepped to the table and rested my hands on the back of the chair before me.

'I'll fetch it out. Anders found it in one of his snares this morning. He has shown Nicky how to make one.'

I nodded, Coop coming to mind and the sight of his body caught in one of his own traps still a vivid memory. 'I have shown him before,' I stated, trying to dispel the gruesome image.

'Have you? He seemed not to know and made no comment.'

'Maybe he has forgotten,' I replied, wondering if our son had feigned innocence in order to gain greater attention from Anders. The idea brought my jealousy to the fore once again, along with regret that he had no father to teach him such things.

'Has Anders done wrong?'

'No,' I replied, shaking my head. 'I just wish Nicholas were here to instruct our son,' I admitted, trusting Marie and being open with her more often than not.

'I understand,' she said, stepping closer and reaching out. 'You miss him by the day,' she stated, placing her hand upon my shoulder, 'as I would miss Anders.'

'Yes,' I responded. 'The wound does not heal and the vacancy does not diminish.'

'It may be that you are not allowing it to,' she said softly.

'What say do I have in it?'

Marie turned me to face her, my hands falling away from the chair. 'There is little I can say, but I am here for you when needed.'

'I know,' I responded, blinking away tears. 'Thank you.'

The door opened and Nicky trooped in wearing his boots, which were caked in mud. Anders followed behind with Honung at his heels.

'What's wrong?' asked Nicky as I averted my gaze.

'Just something in my eye,' I responded as the hound came over and I offered a hand, which it sniffed in greeting.

'Such is the wind today,' stated Anders as he took off his boots and Nicky followed his lead. 'How are you, Chula? Was it good to have the house to yourself?' he enquired with a smile.

'It was… different,' I replied, not wanting to speak about the appearance of the figure nor the loneliness I felt without our son's presence.

He nodded as if comprehending what went unsaid, his smile fading. 'I would feel the same if this house were empty for a night.'

'I hope Nicky has not been any trouble.'

'He is always trouble,' he replied, our son turning to him in surprise. 'The best kind of trouble,' he added, winking at the boy.

Nicky chuckled. 'Another calf has been born,' he stated.

'Marie told me. Have you put it and its mother safely in the barn?'

He nodded. 'And if the last one hasn't given birth by the end of day, we'll be putting it inside too. Anders says it's for the best, until the cold passes.'

'Do you want some help with lunch?' asked Anders, glancing at the vegetables.

'We can do it,' replied Marie.

'What will it be?' Nicky stepped to the table and looked at the raw ingredients.

'A broth,' I replied. 'I am going to add some rabbit meat.'

'From the catch this morning?' he asked, looking up at Marie.

She nodded. 'Maybe you could skin it,' she suggested to her husband.

'Do you want me to teach you how to do that?' he looked down at Nicky, who gave an eager nod of response.

'I'll show him,' I quickly offered, hastening past Marie and to the pantry. 'It is a skill I learnt when I was a girl.'

Stepping into the small room, I saw the carcass hanging from a ceiling hook and reached for it.

'Gjorde jag något fel?' said Anders quietly in his native tongue while I was absent from the room.

'Jag tycker att hon är lite avundsjuk på vår närhet med Nicky ock hon saknar slaven,' replied Marie.

I walked back out, looking to them both and seeing concern in their eyes. I had heard our son's name mentioned in their brief exchange and suspected that the final word meant 'slave.'

'What were you speaking about?' I asked nonchalantly as I stepped to the table and placed the rabbit on top, Honung wandering over and giving the corpse a sniff.

'We were just talking about the calves,' said Marie as her husband patted his knees to encourage the hound away from the table. 'We're worried about the cold.'

I went to the dresser against the back wall and opened the right-hand drawer, taking out a small, sharp knife while Anders crouched and fussed Honung. 'Come over here, Nicky,' I beckoned.

Our son ran his hand along the dog's back and then came around the table to me without enthusiasm.

'Do you want to learn?'

'I want Uncle Anders to show me,' he stated, pouting and keeping his eyes averted.

'I'm sure Ishki will be a good teacher,' he said, scratching Honung behind the ears before rising. 'And maybe it's her turn to teach after I showed you how to set a snare earlier today.'

Our son's cheeks reddened and he glanced up at me guiltily. His reaction informed me that he had not forgotten my instruction in regards the traps, but had done as I suspected; pretended to be ignorant in order to gain the man's attention.

'Will you let me show you how to skin the beast?' I asked, knowing that he would not refuse after he had been found out.

Nicky nodded, but could not hold my gaze.

'Bring over the chair.'

He grasped the back of the chair beside him and brought it over, setting it down next to me.

'You can sit and watch before having a go yourself,' I stated, sliding the rabbit over.

Rain began to drum upon the roof and we all looked up due to the suddenness of the downpour. Turning to the window, I saw the rainfall drawing south, its grey curtain diffusing the landscape that was visible through the frame.

'Shouldn't we go and check on the other cow that is due to give birth?' asked Nicky, trying to use the turn in conditions as an excuse to avoid my guidance.

'I will go with Honung while you learn from your mother,' stated Anders.

'Ishki?' He looked up at me pleadingly.

'If you must,' I conceded eventually.

He ran to the door and put his boots back on before Anders led them outside, the dog rushing by. I stared after him, gaze to the door as it shut.

'What did you and Anders say to each other?' I enquired without turning to Marie, the ears of the rabbit held tightly in one hand and the knife in the other.

'When?' she replied innocently.

'When I was in the pantry.'

I heard her sigh. 'Anders only wondered if he had done something to offend.'

'I heard you mention Nicky's name.'

'That is because I told him that I thought you were feeling a little jealous over our bond with the boy and missing Nicholas.'

'"Slaven",' I quoted.

'Yes, slave.' She passed around to the far side of the table so as to see my face. 'Chula,' she stated, my eyes lifting to hers. 'We said nothing against you and I understand your feelings. He only acts this way due to novelty. We are only sometimes in his life, whereas he has you with him often.

'It is common to overlook those who are closest and to underestimate their importance to us.'

I looked at the tabletop between us, ashamed that I had thought badly of the couple. 'I thought you were speaking ill of me.'

'We would never do such a thing.'

'I know that in truth,' I responded with a sigh. 'I am sorry and you are right, I have been feeling jealous of the way Nicky behaves with you both.'

'Novelty,' she repeated, reaching over the table and resting her hand on mine. 'If it bothers you so, he does not have to stay until the last calf is born, but can return with you.'

I shook my head. 'He should stay and experience the births.'

'So, all is well between us?'

'All is well,' I confirmed.

She smiled with relief and gave my hand a squeeze before letting go. 'I'll see to the vegetables,' she stated as the rain pounded with greater volume, growing heavier still.

'They will be wet through,' commented Marie as she went to the dresser to retrieve a chopping knife.

'Should I fetch out a couple of towels from the storeroom before I bloody my hands?'

'Thank you,' she nodded.

I put the blade down and went into the hallway, opening the door immediately to the right. The store beyond was roughly the same size as the panty, which was located on the other side of the rear wall. Shelves lined the walls and set upon them were household items such as a pan and brush, a couple of lamps and container of oil. At the back were linens, clothes and towels.

I took down two of the latter and draped them over my arm, returning to the main room as Marie began chopping the vegetables. Placing the towels on one of the chairs at the table, I walked over to where the rabbit waited to be peeled. She had placed a board beneath and I smiled at her when she glanced over.

Setting to the task, I made my first cut as the rain drummed and the wind rattled the shutters at the rear of the property. We prepared the meal without speaking, glancing out of the front windows from time to time in expectancy of the men's sodden return.

Marie's knife suddenly fell still. I looked across at her, expecting to find her task completed. Instead, she was swooning, all the colour having drained from her face.

She tottered and started to fall. I dashed around the end of the table in a desperate attempt to catch her before she hit the floor.

Her head smacked violently on the corner of the table, the crack causing me to wince. I reached her and quickly crouched, gathering her to me.

'Marie?' I said softly as blood oozed from the gash at her temple and she lay still in my arms.

* * *

I ran out of the house and into the downpour, leaving the door wide open behind me. Passing around the side of the house, the wind blew rain into my face mixed with hail and I tried to blink away its disturbance in order to locate Anders and Nicky.

I saw them leading a heifer towards the large barn to the left of the corral fifty yards away. 'Hey!' I called, waving my hand as I continued towards them.

They looked over, the Swede's expression becoming one of concern as Honung watched from the doorway to the building, having the sense to find shelter.

'Hurry, get the cart,' I said breathlessly, coming to a halt before them and wiping my eyes, face running with water and forehead filled with pain induced by the sleet and ice cold wind.

'What's wrong?' he asked, glancing past me to the rear of the house.

'Marie has hit her head.'

His eyes widened. 'How?'

'She fainted and banged it as she fell. Ready the cart and bring it to the front. The doctor at the settlement will help.'

I began back towards the house in order to nurse her as best I could. Looking over my shoulder, I saw Anders still standing by the barn, the leading rope in hand and a look of shock upon his face.

'There is no time to lose,' I shouted above the maelstrom.

Passing around to the front of the house, I entered to find her as I had left her; lying unconscious upon the floor. I went to her side, the towel that I had folded and placed to her head thick with absorbed blood.

'Marie?' I said through the loud drumming of the sleet upon the roof, hoping for a response as water dripped to the floor from my hair and face. 'Anders is getting the cart. The doctor at the reservation will see to you.'

Her lids opened a fraction and she looked up at me, face tight with pain. 'Chula?' she asked, blinking as if unable to focus.

'Yes. You fainted and hit your head on the table,' I stated.

Her brow became deeply furrowed as the throb of her injury made itself known to her waking mind. She paled and gagged.

Turning Marie on her side, she vomited onto the boards, the expulsion mainly bile which steamed as its smell was wafted by the strong breeze passing through the room. She convulsed again, her mouth wide, but nothing coming forth apart from a strangled sound caused by the constriction of her throat.

I turned to the sound of boots on the porch and saw Nicky come to an abrupt stop in the doorway, Honung entering and moving to sniff the bile on the boards. He stared at Marie and his nostrils flared against the smell of her outpouring.

'Fetch a cloth from the store room,' I instructed.

'Is she…?'

'She will be fine. Now, do as I say and then bring over the pail of water by the stove.'

He stared a moment longer and then hurried across the room, muddy prints left in his wake. Quickly returning with a pale yellow cloth, he brought it to me and then fetched the pail, struggling with its weight and placing it beside me before moving away, looking upon Marie fearfully.

Her convulsions seemingly ended, I lay her on her back and took the bloodied cloth from her temple. I set about cleaning the gash, which was deep and would need stitches. Water ran down the sides of her head, coloured by diluted blood as I used my thumb to rub away that which had dried about the rent flesh.

'Can you get another cloth?' I requested, glancing back at our son as he stood in stunned silence.

He made no movement, eyes fixed on Marie.

'Nicky!'

He turned to me, eyes glistening.

'Fetch another cloth,' I repeated as Marie groaned.

He hesitated and then left the room, soon coming back and handing me a pale piece of cotton. I folded it into a pad and held it to Marie's temple, the blood flow having almost stopped.

The creak of the cart drew my gaze to the left-hand window and I saw Rödbeta pass outside. 'Anders is here,' I said to Marie.

He stepped in, expression tense and filled with concern as he stared at his wife.

'You can use my fur to help protect her from the sleet,' I stated, glancing at it as it hung from one of the pegs by the door. 'Can you help me get her up?'

He quickly moved to the other side of Marie, balking at the sight of the head injury as we raised her into a sitting position and the cloth fell to her lap. She opened her eyes and looked to him.

'Anders,' she breathed, a faint smile upon her lips.

'You will be okay,' he stated, his voice wavering.

She managed a shallow nod.

With arms about her, we got her up. She tried to stand, but her legs had no strength, knees buckling. The sudden increase in weight caused Anders and I to sink momentarily as we struggled to keep her upright. Straightening, we began towards the door, Marie attempting to move her feet.

'Why are your clothes damp?' she said, her voice enfeebled.

'Sleet,' replied Anders.

She turned to her husband with a look of confusion, her eyes barely open and without focus.

'Snöblandat regn,' he said.

'Oh,' she responded with a vague nod, 'jag förstår.'

'What did she say?' I asked, looking around her.

'I see,' he stated as we reached the doorway.

'Can you pass my fur, Nicky?' I looked to our son, who was watching from beside the table.

He came over and took it from the hook, having to stand on tip toes to do so.

'Thank you,' I said as he passed it to me and I took it in my free hand. 'Can you take her weight while I put it about her shoulders?' I asked Anders.

He nodded and braced himself.

Removing my arm from around Marie, I quickly secured the cloak as best I could, Anders' arm remaining beneath.

Walking out onto the porch, we discovered the sleet had been replaced by thin rain, the activity and focus of our thoughts within the house causing us not to notice the diminishing of the drumming on the roof. We took her around to the rear of the low-sided cart and Anders bent, taking his wife into his arms and lifting her onto the bed of the vehicle.

Climbing on beside her, he moved Marie further away from the open back and she groaned in response. 'Can you bring a pillow?' he said, looking down at me as Honung jumped up to join him, sniffing Marie's face.

I made my way back into the house and went to their room. The shutters were quiet, the wind having died away with the passing of the squall. Taking up one of the pillows on the bed, I quickly made my way back to the rear of the cart and passed it up to Anders.

Placing it beneath his wife's head, he climbed over the front panel and onto the driver's bench. Taking up the reins, he gave them a snap and Rödbeta set off.

Anders turned the cart southward. With another snap, the horse picked up its speed, beginning to cantor as the cart rocked and creaked.

I stood and watched, glancing to my side as Nicky joined me. 'She'll be fine,' I said, as much to myself as to our son as I rested a hand upon his shoulder.

* * *

'We had better get undressed before we catch a chill,' I said after ushering Nicky into the house.

He began to undress as I went to the store room and took a couple of blankets and a large towel from the shelving. I had considered taking him home, but wanted to make sure Marie was all right upon their return.

Going back to the main room, I hung the blankets over the nearest chair and took off my damp dress. The britches followed with a slight struggle. Standing naked and shivering, I briefly dried my skin and then wrapped one of the blankets about me as Nicky took the towel and followed suit.

Picking it up from where he dropped it, I beckoned him over. He stepped closer and I rubbed his hair dry as he looked to the window.

'Do you think she'll be okay?'

'Yes,' I replied, placing the towel back over the chair. 'If you finish chopping the vegetables, I will see to the rabbit. I am sure they will be pleased to arrive home to warm food.'

'I'm cold,' he complained, holding the blanket tightly about him.

'I will light the stove and move the remaining vegetables to that side of the table so the heat will warm you,' I said, moving to the oven and opening the front door.

He sniffed and wiped his nose with the back of his hand while watching me light the fire. The flames took to the kindling and small timbers with ease and warmth was soon radiating out of the open door.

'There you go,' I stated, stepping aside and Nicky quickly moving before it, bending slightly so that he could feel its growing heat upon his face.

Taking our clothes from where they were piled on the floor, I draped them over a chair and moved it closer to the stove in the hope they would soon dry. Picking up the board with the rabbit and skinning knife upon it, I moved it to the end.

'You can sit nearest to the stove,' I stated, placing the vegetables that were still in need of cutting at his intended position.

Seating myself on the chair before the carcass, I took up the knife. Nicky made no move to begin with the chopping and I let him be, knowing from my own experience how cold he was feeling. My extremities were almost numb and my toes were painful with it, paradoxically feeling as though they were on fire.

I tried to focus on the task to distract myself from the discomfort and my worries about Marie, only the vaguest touch of the fire's warmth reaching me. The knife sliced and I skinned the beast, pulling the fur away with a tug as I gripped its rear legs.

Deftly cutting meat from the bone, I piled it on the edge of the board, putting the choice organs nearby by which to make the stock that would become the base for the broth.

Nicky turned to the table, still sniffing as he took up the large knife.

'Be careful of your fingers,' I warned, glancing over at him.

He took the large beet in the centre of the small pile of vegetables and rested it directly before him. Sticking the point in, he sliced down, a slimy trail of mucus snaking from his left nostril.

We proceeded with our tasks without speaking. His sniffing persisted and each time he wiped his nose with the back of his hand, his movements become more agitated as the affliction began to frustrate him.

Finishing before him, I rose and placed larger logs onto the fire in the stove. Lingering beside but careful not to block the growing heat, I crouched and held out my free hand, the other keeping the blanket about my shoulders.

'Do you want me to finish them?' I asked, looking to his profile and seeing his displeasure.

Nicky nodded.

The need to speak to our son about the journal came to the fore of my mind as I looked at him and saw the echoes of your face in his features. 'Come here,' I said softly, gesturing for him to approach with my finger as I remained upon my haunches.

Nicky moved to stand in front of me.

'I know you have been reading the journal,' I stated.

He glanced at me in alarm before turning his gaze to the floor. 'I'm sorry,' he said, fearful of a reprimand.

'You should have asked.'

'Would you have let me read it?' He glanced up again.

I sighed. 'Not yet,' I admitted. 'I was going to wait until you were a few years older.'

'I wanted to know more about my father,' he said sadly.

My heart reached out to him and I cupped his face with my free hand, raising his eyes to mine. 'I would have told you if you had asked me.'

'But you never seem to want to talk about him.'

'It is a hard subject for me to discuss,' I stated, stroking his cheek with the backs of my fingers.

'Did your father really kill him?'

I lowered my hand and looked to the flames visible through the open door of the stove. 'Yes,' I whispered with regret.

Turning my attention back to him, I found his expression to be one of distress. 'Was it the journal that gave you nightmares?'

His frown deepened and he looked to the floor again. 'Are you angry with me?'

Resting my hands upon his shoulders, the blanket slipped to the floor as I looked into his eyes. 'No,' I answered firmly.

'Are you sure?'

'Certain,' I replied before releasing him and taking up the blanket. 'Do you have any questions about your father?' I asked as I wrapped it about me once again.

He pondered a moment before shaking his head. 'I can't think of any.'

'If you do, then do not be afraid to ask.'

Nicky nodded and looked to the door, beginning to move from one foot to the other. 'I need the privy.'

I glanced out of the window, seeing that the drizzle persisted. 'Can you hold it in?' I asked, feeling that enough had been said on the matter of the journal and the past, for the time being at least.

He shook his head. 'I've been holding it in since seeing Marie on the floor.'

I looked to the pegs by the door. Her coat was hanging there and I thought it wouldn't hurt for him to use it.

'Here,' I said, reaching forward. Taking the upper corners of the blanket hung about his neck, I twisted and tied them beneath his chin. 'Put on Marie's coat as well,' I instructed, 'and be as quick as you can.'

Standing, I watched him take the coat down and exit the house. Seeing his head pass the left-hand window, I then set about the task of making the stock for the broth, my thoughts turning to Marie as I wondered at her condition and if the doctor would allow her to return home.

* * *

It was late-afternoon and the rain had passed, though the cloud remained heavy and threatening. The broth simmered on the hotplate in a large cast iron pot as we sat waiting at the table, the temperature in the room having risen considerably and the chill no longer apparent. We were dressed in our clothes once again, the sensation of putting them on having been savoured by both of us, the garments having been dried and warmed by the fire in the stove.

Our son's sniffing had decreased and then stopped altogether, my fear that he may have caught a cold vanishing with it. We had said little, both caught up in thoughts of the past and the Olsens, hoping they would soon return and we would find Marie in good health.

'Do you want to come home with me today?' I asked, looking over at Nicky as he sat with his back to the stove.

'There's still another calf to be born,' he replied.

'It may be that it would be best for Uncle Anders and Auntie Marie,' I responded. 'She has suffered a nasty knock to the head and needs to look after herself.'

He frowned and stared at the tabletop. 'I want to stay,' he stated, scratching the wood with the nail of his forefinger.

'It may be you can, but if Marie is too weakened or otherwise affected, you must be prepared to come back with me and without fuss.'

He glanced up at me. 'Do you think she will be?'

'There is no way of knowing until they return. It may even be that she will stay in the settlement overnight.'

'Really?' he asked with apparent disappointment.

I nodded. 'The doctor may think she should not travel, but should rest up for a while.'

'But she travelled there.'

'Because she was in need of medical attention,' I replied. 'I am only trying to prepare you for what may be so that you do not set your heart on staying.'

He hung his head again and his nail dug at the wood. 'You don't want me to stay.'

'That is not true,' I stated, knowing my words to only be a half-truth. Part of me was happy for him to remain with the Olsens, but another part wanted him home with me.

'Anders has promised to let me ride by myself tomorrow,' he said, his expression increasingly downcast.

'And it may be you still can, even if that means we return in the morning,' I replied, trying to placate him.

Nicky hung his head in sullen silence.

He suddenly looked up and stared towards the door a moment. 'They're home!' he exclaimed loudly, giving me a start and quickly slipping from the chair.

He made his way to the door as I strained to hear any evidence of approach, initially hearing nothing as Nicky opened it. The faint creak of the cart came to me as I looked to the grassland beyond our son. In the distance was the dark shape of the horse and wagon, the silhouette of Anders at the reins, but no sign of Marie.

Pushing my seat back, I got up and went over, gently ushering Nicky onto the porch so that I could shut the door behind us and keep the heat in. We waited, the distance closing with excruciating slowness.

His impatience winning out, Nicky stepped to the grass, his feet bare as he hurried to meet the cart, which was still fifty yards away. Anders pulled on the reins, bringing it to a temporary halt.

Nicky drew alongside and the Swede waved him up to the front bench, our son nimbly climbing aboard and sitting beside him. Taking up the reins, Anders gave them a snap and Rödbeta continued to pull the cart towards the house as Nicky looked into the back.

I remained in place and could see Marie's head and shoulders between Anders and our son. The fact that she was sitting up was a good sign and my sense of relief was immense.

'Hejsan,' greeted Anders as he drew the cart to a stop before the porch.

'I hope you do not mind that we stayed at the house,' I said, stepping down. 'I thought you would like some hot food when you got home and wanted to see if Marie was all right.'

'Take a look for yourself,' he said with a surprisingly bright smile.

Looking at him curiously for a moment, I moved to the rear of the cart. Marie was sitting with her back to the panel behind the driver's bench, the pillow giving her a little comfort and Honung resting beside her, the hound raising her head and regarding me.

'Hej Chula,' she greeted cheerily, her eyes filled with affection, the colour returned to her face and only the bandage about her head hinting at what had happened.

She got to her feet without difficulty, walking to the rear as Anders joined me and Honung padded over. He offered her his hand and helped her down to the grass, the hound leaping down and coming over to sniff my britches.

I saw tears in her eyes as she held my gaze briefly. Overcome with emotion, she stepped close and flung her arms about me.

I raised my arms and held her in return, wondering at the display and thinking it was one of gratitude.

She placed her hands upon my shoulders and looked into my eyes. 'I am pregnant,' she stated softly, tears of joy rolling down her cheeks.

'You…' I looked at her in shock, words failing me.

She nodded. 'The doctor is certain and it is the reason for my fainting.' She smiled and shook her head. 'I can scarcely believe it.'

I glanced at Anders, finding him looking at his wife adoringly, Nicky at his side as Honung sniffed about our feet.

'We are going to have a child,' she stated, barely able to speak as the tears flowed freely.

She took me into her arms once again. I felt her sobbing against me as my heart swelled with gladness.

'I cannot have dreamt of better news,' I said as we continued to embrace, my own tears beginning to fall as I shared in their elation.

* * *

Agent Thompson supervised as we unloaded the last of the rations, carrying sacks of flour over our shoulders that would later be divided into smaller parcels and handed out to those abiding at the reservation. The rain that had filled the cavernous interior with its thunderous drumming had ceased. Only a thin drizzle fell, though the wetness of my coat bore testament to the downpour and my shirt clung to my skin beneath.

The drivers of the wagons had gathered together by one of the vehicles that had already been emptied and drawn up to the side of the building. They were huddled together as they passed around a bottle and smoked, paying us no heed and offering no help.

I paused after placing the sack onto one of the shelving units in the centre of the Exchange. Lifting the front of my hat, I scratched my forehead.

'There's still more to do,' stated Thompson, having noticed my brief respite.

I nodded, securing my hat and walking back to the waiting wagon. Mark passed in the opposite direction and rolled his eyes at me in silent comment of the Agent's constant badgering.

I righted the next sack and grasped a corner with both hands, heaving it over my shoulder. With back bent, I made my way across the earth floor, wincing with the pain induced by the repetition of the task.

The two men whose company I'd once sought when drinking were starting to slack, their feet dragging. We'd unloaded fifteen wagons, a couple of the law officers coming to help for a while when the weather was at its worst and hampering our efforts, Agent Thompson determined that the rations should be unloaded quickly.

A number of residents had gathered about the loading bay doors despite unfriendly looks from the wagon drivers. They'd held out their hands in pleas for food or asked directly, begging us for grain, flour, sugar, cod liver oil or anything else we may be able to give them. Thompson had tried to dissuade them on a number of occasions, but each time he shooed them off with his threats, they ended up returning, like wasps to syrup.

A few still lingered, but most had given up, returning to their homes shivering and soaked through. My feelings of guilt at having to ignore and refuse added to the tension in my muscles. Though the pace of the work made for weariness, I was happy that we were almost done and would soon be free of Thompson's hawk-like presence.

The last sacks were unloaded, the drivers outside dispersing and making their way to their wagons. I rolled my head on my shoulders as the Agent went to the doors and watched the convoy form up and move off to join the main street.

'Shut the doors,' he ordered, looking at me as he turned and made his way towards the desk where people would take their ration tickets during the coming days.

My frown deepened, thinking that he could have seen to the task while there, but making no complaint. Moving the rocks that had kept them in place against the walls, I closed the doors and put the heavy bar in place.

The other men were gathered before the desk, Thompson having taken a small strongbox from the bottom drawer on the far side. I walked over to join them, standing to the rear as the Agent took a key from his pocket and unlocked it.

We waited as he sorted four meagre piles of coins. 'Your payment,' he said with a nod towards them, not deigning to pick them up and pass them out to us.

The others reached for a pile each, moving away from the desk as I stepped forward and took up the last.

'There'll be more work for you tomorrow,' stated Thompson as he closed and locked the strongbox. 'The rations will need to be weighed and apportioned.'

I spread the coins upon my palm with my index finger, looking across the desk at him with eyebrows raised.

'You have something to say about the pay?' he challenged condescendingly, knowing that jobs were relatively scarce and none of us would dare protest for fear of not being hired again.

I shook my head.

'Good,' he stated. 'Make sure you're all here early or others will be chosen to take your place,' he said loudly.

I followed the other men of the reservation to the door that led out onto the main street, hearing Agent Thompson's steps behind me, the officer who'd been present much of the day having left when we'd started unloading the last wagon. Stepping out, I saw my nephew and two nieces who were old enough for school walking eastward towards the edge of the settlement, their education having finished for the day.

Thompson locked the door and strode away in the same direction as the children, making for the administration building and soon stepping out of sight. I stood with back slightly bent, rubbing at its lower reaches to try and ease the stiffness and pain.

Seeing Simon lash out at Celia, I opened my mouth to admonish him, preparing to follow after them in order to help my brother with the fencing. No words came forth as I stared at their backs, seeing Helena sharply clip the boy about the back of the head as punishment. An idea had come to the forefront of my mind and stilled my tongue, causing me to look across at the side street that would take me to the northern fringes of the settlement.

'Chula,' I muttered to myself, my pulse increasing as I began to cross the street.

***

Marie put her spoon down and rested a hand on her stomach as she reclined against the back of the seat. 'Thank you.' She smiled across at me, the pale bandage about her head showing no evidence of blood.

'I am glad you liked it,' I responded, my own small helping already consumed.

Anders reached forward and tore off a piece of bread, using it to wipe up the last of his broth. Nicky glanced at him and tried to stretch for the loaf, Marie having to move it closer so that he could take a piece for himself, our son straining slightly against the tough crust and tearing it loose with a jolt.

I smiled at the sight of him copying the Swede, my jealousy vanquished by the news that the couple were due to have their own child. His adoration for his honorary uncle and aunt was well placed, I thought, for they were good people.

'I should be on my way,' I stated after Anders and Nicky had finished, glancing out of the window, the cloud-veiled sun low in the western sky. 'Is Nicky still permitted to stay until the last of the calves is born?'

Marie and Anders shared a glance, the latter reaching out and resting his hand on hers affectionately.

'His continued company would be very welcome,' replied Marie with a smile.

'Can I ride by myself tomorrow?' he asked enthusiastically.

'I see no reason why not,' responded Anders.

'Did you hear that, Ishki?' He turned to me. 'I'm going to be riding Rödbeta,' he stated, his expression beaming. 'What was it called again, hostridening?'

Anders grinned. 'Hästridning,' he corrected.

'I heard,' I nodded in response to our son. 'Just make sure you keep your mind to the task and do not get over excited.'

'We don't want to be paying the doctor another visit with a broken arm or leg,' added Anders.

'Could I ride her in the morning after we get up?' he looked across at the Swede expectantly.

'After we have eaten and seen to the chores. The animals need their food just as much as we.'

'I'm going give the barnkammare a good clean in the morning,' stated Marie, her use of the term for the spare room gladdening me.

'The doctor thinks the birth is still six months away as yet,' said Anders, 'and you shouldn't push yourself too much after what happened today.'

Marie turned her hand in his and took hold, looking at her husband lovingly. 'And we have waited many years besides,' she replied. 'Six months is nothing more than a tick of the clock and I will make sure to rest if faintness comes over me again.'

They stared into each other's eyes and I saw the glisten of tears, as I had on a number of occasions since they had returned. I thought of the way we had once looked at each other, my love, and my heart ached. In those moments, my feelings of loss were so intense. It was as if your life had been spent only the day before.

I stood abruptly. 'I really should be going,' I stated, walking over to the door and bending to put on my boots, turning my back on the others as I tried to blink away the tears that threatened to fall in your memory.

'There is some honey cake, if you'd stay a little longer,' said Marie.

I shook my head, swallowing back as I straightened and reached for my cloak. 'It will soon be dark,' I stated simply, the emotion clear in my voice as I remained facing the door.

'Is all well?' she enquired.

'Fine,' I said with a fleeting glance.

'Let me wrap some for you.' She released her husband's hand and began to rise.

'I can have some tomorrow,' I said while opening the door. 'If there is anything left after Nicky has had his servings,' I added, forcing a smile as I looked back at them briefly.

'Our thanks for waiting and for seeing to the broth,' stated Anders.

'It was the least I could do.'

'See you tomorrow,' said Marie.

I stepped out of the door and heard quick steps behind me. Turning, I found Nicky fast approaching. He opened his arms wide and hugged me, his head reaching my chest.

'Goodbye, Ishki,' he said against me. 'See you tomorrow.'

I put my hand to the side of his head as we parted, bending to kiss his cheek, but unable to articulate my feelings as I fought to contain my emotions. He looked at my eyes questioningly, noting the gathering of tears, but I turned away and stepped out of the house before he could put voice to an enquiry.

'See you all tomorrow,' I said over my shoulder.

Closing the door, I quickly walked away across the grassland. Every fibre of my being craved your presence and mourned your absence. Just to feel your hand about mine would have been such sweet delight.

A stream of tears ran down my face as I walked through the early evening of long shadows. The cold of the day was deepening as night drew close and the force of my outpouring combined with the chill touch of the breeze to make me tremble with surprising violence.

Gritting my teeth and trying to stem the flow that obscured my vision, I walked with head bowed. There was no solace to be had in those solitary steps, no light to be seen in the darkness within. You had brought illumination and warmth to my heart, my love, my sun.

Nicky's face came to mind. He was the expression of our love and in him it would live on. There was my solace and there was my saving grace. Without him I would have been adrift, but motherhood had kept me anchored despite the turbulence of your passing.

The thought that one day our son would leave filled me with dread. Though I wished him happiness more than anything, I could not bear the thought of losing him to a wife or his independence. Someday I surely would, but I hoped that day would be a long time coming.

'Nothing more than a tick of the clock,' I said, repeating Marie's words to Anders.

That is how much time I felt had passed since Nicky had been born, and yet he was fast becoming a young man. In another tick he would leave and I would be left alone in the house with only memories as my companions. In another tick…

* * *

I reached the southern end of the vale in the dusk. My fur pulled tight about me in the chill, I made my way in thoughtful silence, my pace slow as I thought of the dark emptiness that waited at the cottage.

The barn drew up before me, both it and the nearby trees filled with shadows. I passed it on the eastern side, not wishing to glimpse your grave.

The house came into view and I drew to a sudden halt with heart racing. Narrowing my eyes and wondering if my mind were playing tricks, I peered at the figure standing before the front door. It looked to be the same man that had visited the previous two nights, though less stooped as he rapped on the door, the sound sharp in the hush.

I crouched when he looked over his shoulder, moving to the concealment of the young trees. He went to the window, looking in and making some comment to himself.

Stepping to the path, he walked towards the gate as I considered confronting him.

With heart pounding, I slowly stood up. 'Who are you?'

He stopped with his hand resting on the top bar of the gate and looked over. 'Chula?'

'Who are you?' I demanded with greater volume.

'Hashi.'

I stared at his dark shape in surprise. 'From the settlement?'

'Yes.'

'Why have you been coming here?'

There was a slight hesitation before his reply, his face hidden in shadow. 'I wanted to see you.'

'I am an outcast,' I responded, voice softening.

'I know.'

'Then why would you wish to see me?'

'I...' He took a steadying breath. 'I was curious.'

'I am not a curiosity for your entertainment,' I replied, heat rising in my words.

'That's not what I meant.'

'What did you mean?'

'When I saw you in town…' He struggled to find words again. 'When I saw you, I was struck by your beauty.'

'Are you mocking me?'

'No.' His reply was firm.

I felt my cheeks redden and it was my turn to struggle for a suitable response. 'You must go,' was all I could think of to say.

'It's been a long day. Can't I come in a while and warm myself before returning.'

'I do not know you.'

'Then get to know me,' he responded with growing confidence.

'You would risk banishment from the Nation?'

'To discover if you are the woman I think you to be, yes.'

'And what woman is that?'

'One of beauty to my eyes and appeal to my heart,' he replied, 'and one who adheres to the old ways.'

I did not know how to respond. I could not entertain the thought of being pursued by him or any other man. With my loss so close, I wanted distance between me and any amorous interest. There was also another fear that I was loathe to admit; that the stirring I had felt upon our first meeting would return.

I was suddenly overcome with the sensation that you were watching, my love. It was a test of my continuing love for you and my loyalty.

'You must leave,' I stated, wishing to be free of him and to display that I was still yours.

'I only ask for a little time and a little warmth before the fire.'

'There is no fire and I will not be lighting it before I am to my bed,' I replied. 'Now, please leave.' I was feeling increasingly discomforted, my body filled with tension as I willed him away from our home.

Hashi continued to stand with his hand on the gate as the gloom of dusk deepened into night, mist thickening about us now that the wind had died away. 'Can I call again? Tomorrow, maybe?'

'No. I am an outcast and it would not fare well for you if your visits were found out,' I replied. 'Stay away from the farm and do not linger in the woods nearby. There are traps still hidden about the vale that could cause you injury and even death,' I added despite the fact I was sure all of Coop's traps had been found, hoping that he would think twice about ignoring my instructions.

Hashi opened the gate and stepped through. 'I understand,' he said, his voice conveying his disappointment.

He began to walk in my direction and I slunk back into the embrace of the trees, watching him with heart thumping.

'Anowa chipisala' cho,' he stated as he walked past through the darkened mist.

'We will not meet again,' I stated in response to his words, which meant 'until we meet again' in our native tongue.

Waiting until he had vanished from sight, I made my way out of the trees and towards the house. Regularly looking over my shoulder, the thought occurred that he had not left, but was lurking somewhere in the misty night.

The hairs on the nape of my neck arose in response and my pace increased. Passing through the gate, I hurried up the path to the door and entered, closing it and fastening the simple latch.

Going to the window, I peered out with my hand above my eyes to eliminate the disturbance of my reflection. I could barely see the boundary fence, the young trees hidden from sight.

I closed and secured the shutters, the room pitch black. Knowing my way around after years of abiding there, I fetched out a lamp and a couple of matches, lighting it and turning up the wick to chase away the darkness.

Going to the fire, I prepared and lit it. The combined light of the flames and lamp helped to calm me a little as I sat on the edge of the nearest seat. Keeping the fur about my shoulders, I waited for the warmth to penetrate, my thoughts returning to Hashi with disturbing regularity.

I felt like a traitor in those long minutes, my love. Part of me wanted him to disobey my instruction and return. I wanted to hear a knock at the door and to find him standing on the threshold. And with every thought of him, I felt I betrayed you.

* * *

The night was deep by the time I arrived back at my brother's farmstead. I entered to find only he, Emily and Helena still up, seated on stools before the fire.

'Did you find work today?' asked Duncan, looking to my eyes to discern whether or not I'd been drinking as I walked over to the fire to warm myself.

'I was one of those picked to unload the ration wagons,' I replied, holding my hands towards the flames between him and Emily.

'You've finished late,' she commented, trying to fish out the truth of where I'd been since leaving the Exchange.

'I haven't been drinking,' I stated flatly, pulling over a stool and seating myself to the left of the family. 'Where's Simon? He's usually still up.'

'A disagreement with Celia caused him to be sent to his bed without supper,' stated Helena, her back straight and a housedress draped over her lap as she mended a hole.

'I wasn't accusing,' said Emily softly. 'We had been wondering where you'd got to.'

'I went for a walk, is all.'

I glanced at Duncan and knew what he was thinking, but he didn't want to ask the question in front of his wife and child.

'Is there more work for you tomorrow?' he asked.

I gave a nod, looking to the flames and thinking about Chula. 'They will be apportioning the rations and if I am there early, then I will be one of those chosen for the task.'

'I'll be sure to wake you,' said Emily.

'Will you be moving back to your farm soon, Uncle Andrew?' asked Helena without looking up as she sewed.

'What she means is,' began Emily, worried that her daughter's words may offend, 'you could still be putting in seeds and reaping a harvest, so it may be a good idea to move back sooner rather than later.'

'I don't know,' I responded to the girl.

She glanced up, a frown on her face. I was well aware of her feelings towards me, ones which I couldn't blame her for after months of causing drunken disturbance in the household. There'd been one occasion when I'd burst into the girl's room, Celia and Helena sharing. It had been late and in my intoxicated confusion, I'd barrelled through the wrong door, stumbling and knocking into their beds. They'd woken and Celia had been reduced to tears as I blustered incomprehensibly, falling to the floor and vomiting on the boards.

If Emily had had her way, I'd have been thrown out that night, but Duncan had seen to me and in the morning they'd sat me down and given me a final warning. The girls' reluctance to have anything to do with me afterwards, along with the words of my brother and his wife, had helped me make the decision to start down the hard path to sobriety.

'You seem a little distracted this evening,' commented Emily.

'Pardon?' I turned to her.

'Duncan said he'd help with the planting and any repairs that may be needed to your property.'

'I'm not sure I can ever go back,' I responded.

'You cannot mourn for the rest of your life.'

'I do not mourn, I remember, and that place is filled with memories.'

'Make some new ones,' stated Helena matter-of-factly.

I glanced at the girl as she pulled the needle through the thick material.

'She's right, you know,' said Emily. 'The best way to dispel the old ones is to create new. You have started to rebuild your life and there is no reason to stop now.'

'It's not that we want to throw you out,' interjected Duncan quickly.

'I know,' I nodded. 'With the other baby on the way there will be no room for me. I promise you, I will leave before it is born.'

'But that's another seven months!' exclaimed Helena, looking unhappily at her mother.

Emily frowned at her daughter, her expression tight and showing her displeasure at the minor outburst. 'She doesn't mean anything by it,' she said apologetically, looking past her daughter, who stared sourly at her needlework.

'Yes, she does, and I don't blame her,' I responded, wishing there were some way to mend the rift between me and the girls.

Oka and Helena had once enjoyed a strong bond, playing together at a time when Celia had only just learnt to walk. My relationship with both Helena and Simon had been a good one, filled with horseplay and laughter, but my laughter had ended with the death of my family. I'd thought my desire and ability to love had also died with them, but Chula was making me question this belief. She was awakening something that had not passed away, but had merely been slumbering in the broken and cold depths of my heart.

'I think it's time I was to my bed,' stated Emily, rising to her feet after she and my brother shared a look of silent communication. She placed a hand on her daughter's shoulder. 'Come on, young lady, you too.'

'But I haven't finished yet,' moaned Helena.

'The dress can wait until morning.'

Helena glanced unkindly at me, as if knowing her repairing had been curtailed on my account. Standing, she placed the dress on the stool. 'Celia and Simon better not interfere with it when they get up.'

'I'll see to it that they don't,' responded Emily as Duncan got to his feet and placed more wood on the fire. 'Now, off to bed with you.' She gave the girl a gentle push on the back.

'See you in the morning,' she said in parting, following her daughter out of the room.

Duncan retook his seat and looked over his shoulder to check that Emily and Helena had vacated. 'Did you seek out the outcast?' he asked with voice lowered.

I nodded without taking my gaze from the flames. 'I went to her farmstead and she asked me to leave.'

'Then she has more sense than you.'

I slowly turned to him. 'Do you want my happiness, Brother?'

'I would see you restored to who you once were,' he confirmed.

'I will never be who I once was, but it may be I can be reborn to love and joy.'

'With the outcast? That it foolishness. How will you find joy when cast out by your own people?'

'My own people,' I echoed, turning back to the fire while shaking my head. 'Where are they?'

'All about you.'

'The reservation is not home to the Chickasaw, but to a Nation under the shadow of the whites. We are slowly changing to be like them.'

'If we don't, then what will become of us? Our hunting lands were taken and we had little choice but to become farmers on the land they provided.'

'We could have fought.'

'And what came of fighting in the past? Would you see us all slaughtered?'

I sighed. 'No.'

'Then we have only one choice.'

'I have more,' I responded.

'To make an alliance with a woman who was prepared to sully her Chickasaw bloodline? Don't you see that she's no friend to our Nation?' said Duncan, hoping the change of tact would appeal to my respect of the old ways. 'She ran away with a slave and in so doing, she betrayed our heritage.'

'She did no such thing,' I responded curtly.

'No? Then what would you call it?'

'If she's the woman I think her to be, then she did so out of love.'

'It is still a betrayal of our Nation.'

I remained silent, the fire crackling before me.

'Promise me you will not visit with her again.'

'I already told you, she asked me to leave and not return,' I stated with growing irritation.

'Then be wise, follow her instruction. Move back to your farmstead and plant seed so that you may harvest, so that you may have a future with our people.'

Again I said nothing.

'Will you promise me, Brother?'

'I will not visit her again,' I stated.

He seemed satisfied that my words held no lie. 'You will see the wisdom of it in time,' he said. 'Now, I must go to my bed. There is much to be done tomorrow.'

Duncan got to his feet and rested a hand on my shoulder, as his wife had done with their eldest child. 'I love you, Brother, and would not see you throw your life away on a woman who follows the whims of her heart above the wishes of her father and laws of her people.'

'Have you never felt such love as would overthrow all you hold true?' I looked up at him.

'Emily and I love each other well, but…'

'There are no buts. I'd have done anything for Jane and Oka, even laid down my life for them.'

'And that is what you have done since their passing,' responded Duncan. 'Do you think they would have wanted you to do so? Go back to the farm and honour their memory by living once more.'

'I cannot,' I protested loudly, snapping my shoulder forward so his hand fell away.

I flexed my fingers as I tried to fight the surge of bitterness and anger, filled with such rage against myself. 'I could do nothing,' I stated, staring at the fire.

'There was nothing you could do.'

'I held Oka in my arms as she died, making false promises that she would be fine, that she would recover.' My eyes became swollen with tears.

'Jane diminished before my very eyes until that fateful day when I found her in the pine wood.'

'You are not to blame for their passing.'

'Then who?' I asked forcefully, turning to look up at him. 'If I could do nothing, if the love I bore for them could have no bearing...' I shook my head, my tears beginning to fall. 'I was helpless.'

'The Good Lord does not reveal His reasons. He gives life and He taketh away.'

'The Good Lord,' I snorted, shaking my head. 'And you would speak to me of our traditions.' I wiped my eyes with the backs of my hands. 'You are like the rest, have released them to the wind like the ashes of our ancestors.'

'You are still my guest,' he reminded with a warning in his tone.

I said nothing in reply.

He stood for a while and then made his way out of the room. I listened to his steps and the sound of the bedroom door opening and shutting.

Sniffing, I wiped my eyes again and blinked away the remainder of my tears. My internal pain was still great, but Chula's face came to mind and had a calming effect. I had loved before and discovered its torment, but maybe it could be different with her.

I'd heard what had happened to her slave, knew that we were kin in our loss. Maybe, if we could kindle a new love together, we would find ourselves fulfilled this time instead of torn apart.

'Chula,' I muttered to the dancing flames, wondering if she too said my name in the night.

Friday, April 11, 1873

I awoke sobbing in the darkness. My cheeks were wet and the moisture brought with it a chill touch, the night deeply cold.

In the dream, I had been in Hashi's arms. There had not been contentment or happiness, only a profound sadness that I was not in your embrace, my love. It was so overwhelming that it was carried from the realm of dreams into reality.

My heart ached as I lay in my cot, my back to the window. There was no sound of wind or rain, only silence. I longed for the nights of late spring and summer when a multitude of creatures would add their sounds to the darker hours. Frogs and crickets would call, night birds would occasionally sing. There would be life, but now there was only memories and silence.

I thought of you, my love. I thought of the time we had danced in the snow. My tears were renewed. Was it wrong to still mourn when it had been so long? I could not let you go, but felt that some small part of me had awakened to the possibility of loving another.

Reaching out from beneath the furs, I groped for the lamp I knew to be on the small table beside my bed. Locating it and the matches beside, I struck one on the frame of my cot. The flame was passed from one to the other. I closed the shutter and turned up the wick, the shadows retreating into the eaves and corners of the room.

I stared at the solitary flame; straight and true within the protection of the glass. I saw your face. I saw our son's. The resemblance was so strong.

The creak of a floorboard in the hallway caused my skin to prickle and I looked at the door to my room with wide eyes. My heart raced as I listened for further sounds, but only felt the silence pressing upon my eardrums.

Pulling back the covers and standing, the cold forgotten, I took hold of the lamp's handle, which squeaked as it swayed in my grasp. I slowly padded towards the door, all the while listening.

Opening it, I held the lamp out into the hall, its light illuminating nothing untoward. I crossed over and opened the door to the room that had been Nicky's until recently, again finding nothing but emptiness.

Going to the main room with growing confidence in my steps, I found it vacant. Shaking my head and admonishing myself for being so easily perturbed, I set the lamp on the mantle above the fire and considered lighting it.

Wondering at the time, I went to the window and unfastened the shutters in order to peer out in search of day's first light. My gaze went immediately to where I knew the gate to be, but the darkness was so complete that I could not see it. I pictured the figure standing there and my brow became creased as a realisation came upon me.

'His coat and hat,' I whispered, my breath misting the pane before me as I tried to picture the figure with greater clarity.

I nodded, certain that I was right. Its coat had been considerably longer than Hashi's and the brim of its hat wider.

I recounted the conversation with Hashi. I had mentioned his visits, but he had not protested that there had been no others. I recalled a hesitation in response and wondered if it could have been caused by confusion.

'It was not him,' I stated to the night, finding no trace of coming day beyond the glass, only my distorted reflection, the darkness of my eyes still containing the sadness with which I had woken.

* * *

I woke again, this time in the seat before the hearth. I had not lit the fire when first rising. Instead, I had gone to my room and collected my bed cover, taking it to the main room and finding fitful sleep before the ashes of the previous night. The woodpile was much diminished and I did not know when I would find time to collect more. I had need to visit my sister and then to go to the Olsens' farm. Further to this, I wondered if I should visit with Hashi to find out if I was indeed correct in my estimation that he had only visited once.

'Maybe Essy knows where he lives,' I said to myself as I stretched and my face briefly contorted.

I got to my feet and went to the window, opening the shutters once again to find a cold grey day beyond. The top of the eastern hill could not be seen, shrouded by thick clouds that passed southward. The sun had yet to rise, but its presence above the vale would make little difference on such an overcast day.

Thinking to break the fast, I went to the food cupboard and peered within, having to narrow my eyes in order to make out what was contained within, such was the gloom. Taking out the stale end of a loaf and the last knob of butter, I fetched a plate and knife from the dresser before sitting to eat the simple meal.

My stomach groaned as I chewed. The crust was hard, scraping against my gums and giving rise to a little blood that stained the stale bread when I bit into it. I stared at it and envisaged you slumped against the tree. The bullet was fast taking your life. It was yesterday and yet another lifetime.

I took a deep breath and continued to eat, turning my gaze to the window. How could I be with another when your presence remained so strong and my love with it?

I shook my head as I watched the dark shape of a bird swoop down from above the house, gliding with speed towards the eastern woodland. The door knocked gently in place, as if the wind wished to gain entry.

I missed our son, but took solace in the fact that he would be home once there were no more calves to be born. I was hopeful that he would accompany me back that day and return the house to its usual vitality.

Finishing the last of the food, I sat back and stared out. Trying to guess the time, I was at a loss. There had been no change in the brightness of the day since I had risen and therefore no clue as to how long I had slept.

Deciding to head into town and knowing its activity would indicate the time of day, I got up, holding the bedcover about me. Taking the plate to the dresser, I rested it on top to be washed later.

I went to my room and placed the cover back on my bed. Taking the dress that I wore in order to blend in when visiting the settlement from where it hung on a hook near the door, I put it on, feeling a chill draught upon my calves.

I went to the front door and put on my boots before donning the hooded cloak I always wore. Taking a final glance about the interior, I stepped out and the wind immediately pulled at my clothing, its low moan filling the vale as it swept along it.

Holding the hood at the neck and with my head bowed, I made my way to the gate. Opening it, my gaze went to the mud on the far side, looking for evidence of fresh footprints, but seeing none.

Making my way south along the vague track, I went to visit with you first. I needed to feel close to you.

Entering the barn through the southern doorway, I saw that a section of the wall beside had fallen, is stones spilling and reaching the foot of your grave. Stepping over them, I went and knelt next to your final resting place, placing my palm to the uppermost marker.

'Chi-hollo-li.'

There was no sense of connection. All I felt was the cold hardness of the stone as the wind swirled around the interior and stirred the high vegetation gathered within the walls.

Closing my eyes, I tried to block out all disturbance, to find the peace I always did when coming to you in the mornings. It did not come.

I stared at the pile of stones. 'Where are you?' I whispered.

The wind moaned and the trees beyond the walls swayed.

'Not here,' I said in answer to my own question.

Feeling saddened by your absence, I withdrew my hand. Standing, I took a breath and turned for the door. Making my way out of the ruin, I decided to leave the chicken coop closed and headed for the settlement, disconcerted by the visit. I had found comfort at your graveside countless times in the years since your passing and the sudden lack left me ill at ease. That comfort, that connection, had been the bedrock of each day. Without it I was left dissatisfied and unsettled.

A few drops of rain patted against my hood as I passed around the foot of the vale, heading southeast. I glanced about me from within the shadow of the hood, expecting to see the figure motionless and watching, but finding nothing but the reflection of my agitation in the movements of the trees.

* * *

I sat on the bench outside the Exchange. Mark was already there and a drunk slept at the far end, long coat covering him and one arm draped over the side, a half-empty bottle lying on the ground just out of reach of his fingers. There was no sign of Agent Thompson despite his instruction to be early.

I hunkered down within the vague warmth of my coat, the wind carrying a chill. My nose was numb and cheeks raw as I waited.

Glancing along the street towards the administration offices, I saw her. I couldn't see her face, but Chula was wearing the same hooded cloak as when I'd first set eyes on her two days before.

Seeing her hurry into an alley, I quickly rose and headed after her. Reaching its entrance, I watched her pass across the street at the other end.

Hastening along the alley, I saw her knock on the side door of one of the houses opposite. 'That's Nathan's place,' I said to myself, having helped him gather the harvest the previous year, my employment foreshortened after arriving so drunk I could barely stand.

The door was opened and she stepped out of sight with a brief backward glance.

My heart pounding, I walked across the street and passed down the passage. Stopping before the door, I leant to the wood and heard faint conversation beyond. Chula was speaking with another woman, though the words were spoken too softly to be made out.

I looked back to the street. There was no one in sight.

I lifted my hand to knock, the promise that I'd made to my brother in regards not visiting with Chula coming to mind. There had been no such oath relating to speaking with her in the settlement and I felt no guilt, only nervousness and excitement as the prospect of seeing her face caused my hands to tremble slightly.

Rapping on the door a couple of times, I heard shushing inside and steps approaching.

'Who is it?'

'I've come to speak with Chula,' I replied.

'There's no one by that name here.'

'I saw her enter.'

There was the faint sound of whispering.

'Who am I speaking to?' asked the woman.

'Hashi.'

More whispering followed and then the door opened.

Chula was standing beyond a table on the other side of the shadowy room, her hood down and long hair framing her strong features. Her eyes captivated me and I was momentarily held in place.

'Quickly,' hissed the woman who held the door, beckoning me inside.

The spell was broken as I glanced at her before stepping in. She banged the portal shut behind me as I stood facing Chula, finding no words, but nodding a greeting.

'What are you doing here?' she asked with obvious annoyance.

'I was sitting outside the Exchange and saw you,' I replied. 'I wanted to speak with you.'

'Did I not make myself clear yesterday? I do not want anything to do with you, and you should want nothing to do with me. I am an outcast.'

'I know who you are,' I stated, taking a step forward, 'and I care not.'

She shook her head in frustration. 'You must leave and never approach me again, for your own sake.'

'And yet you meet with this woman,' I said, glancing to my left.

'She is my sister.'

I looked to the other woman with greater attention, seeing a slight resemblance.

'Esther,' she introduced.

'Glad to make your acquaintance,' I responded with a shallow bow of my head.

'You cannot stay,' she added. 'There is risk enough without your presence.'

'Agree to see me just once and I will leave,' I said, turning my attention to Chula once again, finding myself drawn to the warm depths of her eyes.

'No good can come of it,' she stated, 'so there is little point.'

'I do not care about your past nor your position.'

She looked at me in bemusement. 'How can you be so certain that I am someone you wish to know?'

'My heart tells me so,' I replied without hesitation, knowing there may not be another occasion to express my desire.

'You know nothing of who I am. I would be a disappointment,' she responded. 'Besides, I have no wish for a man.'

The quick addition of her last words gave me hope. It was as if they were an afterthought, added by a part of her that battled to remain in the throes of yesterday.

'Just one time,' I insisted. 'If your heart holds no warmth for me when it is done, then I'll never approach you again.'

Chula looked to her sister, who shook her head. 'I do not know,' she admitted.

'What harm can it do?'

'If you were seen with me, it could make you an outcast.'

'One time,' I repeated, sensing her closeness to agreement and smiling disarmingly. 'There's nothing for you to lose, but plenty to be gained.'

'One time?'

'Yes.'

She hesitated and then conceded with a nod.

'Chula!' snapped Esther, giving her sister a hard look which was ignored.

'Should I come to your farm?' I asked quickly, worried that she'd change her mind if given the chance to think on her decision too long.

'No,' she stated firmly.

'Then where?'

'Do you have a house?'

My heart sank. 'I... I can't.'

'Then we have nothing more to speak about,' responded Chula, looking to the door.

I glanced over my shoulder, feeling my chance slipping away. 'At mine,' I conceded without enthusiasm. 'When?'

'When I am done here, I will come and visit. Where do you live?'

'My farmstead is west. Take the main track out of the settlement and then the second turning to the right and follow it to its end. The house is set against a pine wood and a stream runs beside it,' I stated, choosing not to tell her that I didn't dwell there anymore, knowing it would lead to further questions that I wasn't willing to endure for the time being.

'West it is,' she stated.

I paused and then stepped to the door. Taking the handle, I turned to Chula as her sister watched with disapproval. 'Anowa chipisala' cho,' I said in parting, forcing a smile.

'Anowa chipisala' cho,' she responded with a slight bow.

I stepped out, the cold wind immediately taking me into its arms as the door was quickly closed by Chula's sister.

* * *

'What do you think you are doing?' demanded Essy angrily.

'What harm can come of it?'

'He could be made an outcast like you,' she snapped back. 'Besides, he's nothing more than a drunk.'

'I did not ask him, but he me,' I replied, not in the mood to have an argument and seating myself at the table.

'You did not have to agree,' she said, moving to stand opposite and glaring down at me as she set her hands on the tabletop. 'Let me go after him and say you've changed your mind.

I shook my head.

'Why are you being so selfish?' she blurted in annoyance. 'He'll be outcast and then you'll never be rid of him. Think on that for a moment and think on how Nicky would feel.'

'I have no need to think on it. Hashi can make his own choices and Nicky is in want of a father figure.'

Essy's mouth hung open. 'You would really consider a union with such a man?'

'I do not know what kind of man he is, as yet,' I said, her verbal assault making me more determined to meet with Hashi.

'You can be headstrong, I know that, but I have rarely known you to be foolish.'

'Rarely?' I raised my eyebrow. 'You mean like when I ran off with Nicholas.'

'What else would you call it?' she challenged.

'We followed our hearts.'

'You followed a whim,' she said cuttingly.

I held her gaze momentarily, controlling my own anger. 'It was love that set me on the path away from home,' I replied, my voice soft. 'It was love for which I was prepared to risk all. If that is foolishness then I am a fool without doubt.'

'Love.' She shook her head. 'You were too young to know what it was. Don't you see now that it was obsession?'

I did not answer, my hands gripped tight upon my lap and nails digging into my skin as I tried to suppress the rage that was building. 'Say no more, Essy,' I stated, my words filled with warning.

'And that is always your way,' she continued, her own feelings carrying her on. 'Whenever the subject is broached you dismiss it. You hide from the truth in favour of the lie that you have been telling yourself for over eight years.'

'Lie!' I suddenly stood, the chair propelled backwards and smacking into the wall. 'You call the love I shared with Nicholas a lie!' I seethed, hands balled into fists at my sides. 'Just because you have never known such love does not mean it is a lie.'

'I know love and I know the difference between love and obsession. What else would you call visiting his grave every morning? What else would you call pining after him after all this time when even people who have been together all their lives do not mourn this long?'

I stared at her and she at me.

Without another word, I stormed around the table and to the door. Flinging it open as tears began to fall, I fled the heat of our exchange. Pulling the hood over my head, I stalked up the passageway without pause, the sound of the door slamming in my wake causing me to wince.

* * *

I walked up the track filled with apprehension. I hadn't been back to the farmstead since finding Jane's body hanging in the pine wood. I'd taken her down and carried her into town, falling to my knees on the main street and wailing uncontrollably.

I had no idea what state it would be in and didn't want to know in truth. But it wasn't its condition that filled me with sickness, it was the memories I feared would be stirred by my going back there, the ghosts of my wife and daughter already restless as I drew ever nearer.

I walked around a bend, the track passing a rocky outcrop with a sharp drop on the near side. I braced myself, knowing that the farm would come into sight once I'd passed, my pace slowing to a crawl and gaze to the ground.

I lifted my head and forced myself to look ahead. The house rested one hundred yards away, young trees growing at its sides and the pines visible beyond. I could see that the front door was missing and wondered if it were by accident or design as I made myself continue towards it.

The stream I'd mentioned to Chula ran to the left of the house. A low and twisted tree reached out over of the water ten yards ahead of the house, the swing I'd hung from one of the branches still in evidence. It was swaying to and fro, and I imagined Oka's spirit resting there, swinging her legs and smiling brightly. Her laughter was lifted on the wind of my imagination and a shiver ran the length of me.

I reached the front gate at the end of the track. It was stuck open, a thick growth of grass having captured it and woven about the lower bar.

I hesitated before it, staring at the darkness visible through the doorway.

'Hashi!'

The call gave me a start and I turned with heart pounding to find Chula fast approaching.

* * *

My steps faltered as he turned around. Never had I seen someone look so forlorn. His eyes were filled with glistening torment and I wondered what could have possibly befallen him in the short time since I had seen him at my sister's.

'What is wrong?' I asked as I neared, my pulse elevated.

'I've not been here for some time,' he stated, not trying to hide his emotion, but baring it to me, raw and unguarded.

'Why?' my question was barely a whisper as I came to a halt before him.

'You don't know the story?'

I shook my head. 'Essy tells me only what she chooses of life on the reservation.'

'Essy?'

'My sister.'

He nodded to himself. 'My daughter, Oka, passed away from illness. She wasted away in her bed, gripped by terrible coughing that brought on vomiting. After she passed…'

Hashi took a wavering breath, clearly struggling to put words to what had happened. I reached out and took his hand, the touch shocking me almost as much as him, the act automatic and arising out of sympathy.

He looked down at our bond and gathered himself. 'My wife took her own life,' he stated.

'I am so sorry,' I replied, the words falling far short of how I felt in sight of his distress. 'Why did you not say?'

'I didn't wish to answer the questions that would have arisen as a result of saying that I don't abide here.'

'I did not mean to be the cause of such anguish.'

He shook his head and held my gaze. 'It's not your fault and it is different now that your sister isn't present,' he responded. 'I would reveal anything to you.'

I stared into his dark eyes for a moment, looking up at him and feeling the intensity of the emotions within him. 'And I you,' I replied, the admission coming from the depths of me and awakened by the circumstances.

'We can leave,' I suggested.

He shook his head again. 'We are here. With you, I can go on.'

I gave a nod and he turned, passing through the gate, our hands still clasped together. I followed and drew up beside him as we walked through the tangles of long grass which swished against our legs and were rippled by the wind.

* * *

We reached the entrance to the house, the touch of her fingers about mine giving me the strength to enter. The door was on its side and leaning against the front wall, covered in creeping vegetation that was making its way up the sidings.

We went inside and I brought us to a halt. Looking around the interior, I found the main room empty bar a solitary chair in the centre of the room. Leaves were gathered in the corners after having been corralled into the house by the wind. There were thick cobwebs amidst the eaves, some having broken and dusted strands hanging down, bringing to mind the sight of Jane's body in the pine wood.

I swallowed back and my grip on Chula's hand tightened at the thought that the rope still hung there.

'Are you all right?' she asked softly.

I turned to her, barely able to stop myself from collapsing, my grief and anguish threatening to buckle my legs. 'Can we go?'

* * *

I led the way back out of the sorry house, is hollowness in stark contrast to the family life I imagined had once filled it with activity and conversation. Hashi stumbled as he walked behind me and I looked back worriedly, his mental condition weakening his body's resolve to go on.

'I'm okay,' he stated quietly.

We made our way to the gate and I glanced at the swing beside the stream. A symbol of childhood happiness, its presence was incongruous against the backdrop of the empty house and overgrown surroundings.

Passing onto the rough track, Hashi brought us to a stop. I turned and found his cheeks streaked by tears. He took tremulous breaths, trying to control himself so that we might continue away from the place that haunted and tortured him so.

Releasing my hand, he bent double and retched, expelling nothing but air.

'I have also suffered great loss,' I confided as he tried to recover himself.

'The slave.'

'His name was Nicholas,' I stated as he straightened, 'and I loved him dearly.'

'I didn't think I could ever love another.' He looked to me meaningfully.

'You still have no idea who I am.'

'I know enough,' he responded through more deep breaths. 'Enough to know that I wish to be with you and discover all you're willing to reveal.'

'And what of being made an outcast?'

'We felt like outcasts and I still feel that way.'

'You and your wife?'

'Jane,' he said with a nod. 'We held to the old ways, calling our daughter Oka because of the stream.'

'Water,' I stated.

Despite his state, Hashi managed a gentle smile. 'Indeed,' he replied. 'We saw many in the Nation adapting to the ways of the whites, whether voluntarily or by coercion. I've been an outsider for many years, so being declared an outcast holds little sway.'

'What if you discover I am not who you think me to be?'

'You're already more.' He reached out and retook my hand.

I found myself made speechless by the re-establishing of contact and the look of intense desire in his glistening eyes. The wind gusted about us as we stood motionless amidst the motion of trees and grasses.

My gaze was attracted to movement over his left shoulder. A solitary white feather had lifted into view, dancing on the wind. It was the same shape and size as the one I had found in the ruined barn and I suddenly felt you there, felt your approval and imagined you smiling.

My own tears rising to the fore, I leant forward and went up on tip toes, kissing Hashi with the tenderness of release.

* * *

Chula's eyes drew closer as she raised herself to my lips. With that caress I was lost to her.

She lowered herself, a blush to her cheeks that was endearing as she continued to hold my gaze.

'When can I see you again?' I asked in a whisper.

'If you are free this afternoon, you can come to the farmstead.'

I nodded, having no intention of helping at the Exchange. My lips tingled and my heart yearned to feel hers pressed to them once again.

'I must visit with neighbours first,' she said, 'but will return by the middle of the afternoon.'

'There are neighbours who will speak with you?'

'They are not of the Nation. They are Swedish settlers whose claim is just beyond the borders of the land set aside for our people.'

'You still call them "our people",' I observed.

'I will always belong to them, whether they choose to acknowledge that fact or not. They cannot wipe away my heritage or my parentage. My blood is Chickasaw.'

She looked to the house briefly. 'I have a son,' she revealed.

'The sla… Nicholas'?' I enquired.

Chula gave a nod of confirmation. 'I named him after his father.'

'How old is he?'

'Seven.'

Oka came to mind, having been the same age when she passed. 'I look forward to meeting him.'

'Not yet,' she replied with a touch of sharpness. 'He is staying with the Olsens at present,' she added, purposefully softening her tone. 'Some of their cattle are calving and he wanted to be there. The wonder of youth.' She smiled, the expression making me want to take her into my arms.

'Wonder should be a thing of all ages,' I responded, reaching out and touching her hair. 'It is the way by which we see the profound beauty of the world. Through such awe the Great Spirit is sensed. You are a wonder to me.'

She looked to the ground coyly. 'If you say the same when you truly know me, then I will believe it is so.'

She stepped back, the strands falling from my fingers. 'I must leave. The Olsens are expecting me and I have yet to see Nicky today.

'It is best if you linger here awhile so there is no chance that anyone will see us together,' she added over her shoulder, beginning to walk away.

'Anowa chipisala' cho,' I said in parting.

'This afternoon,' she replied with a smile.

* * *

I walked away as if in a daze, thinking his words about wonder were akin so something you might have said. They, along with the emotion he had displayed, revealed there was a depth to the man which held great appeal.

As the distance between Hashi and I grew, so did my surprise. I could barely believe that I had taken his hand and kissed him. As the heightened emotions faded, I began to question my actions, reminding myself that I did not know the man as yet.

Despite the feather seeming like it was a sign, I felt guilt. I had not paid another man any regard since your passing, and within the space of minutes I had shared touches and a caress. There was no denying that my heart lifted with the contact and my stomach was filled with lightness, but those feelings were fast being replaced with the weight of betraying you, my love.

I approached the settlement in order to pass through and make my way north, unsure as to the route from the west side of the town. I pulled my hood up, the continuing wind meaning that I had to hold it beneath my chin in order for it to stay in place. Bowing my head as I passed the first buildings, I tried to remain unknown to those I passed, seeing only the lower portion of their legs in the periphery of my vision.

The solitary leg of a veteran came into view, the empty left side of his britches sewn up and a wooden crutch serving to help him walk.

'Nora?'

There was something about the voice that I recognised and caused the hairs on the back of my neck to rise, the sensation added to by the use of my given name.

I stopped and turned. Lifting my head, my eyes widened in shock, mouth falling open.

Standing not five yards away was my youngest brother.

'Akocha?' I said, my voice barely audible above the rush of wind.

He stared at me with equal disbelief. 'I was told you were dead.'

'And I you,' I replied.

He hopped closer, leaning heavily on the crutch. 'Haven't you a hug for your brother?'

I went to him and held him close. The embrace was tight with heartfelt joy as the two of us stood in the middle of the street for long moments.

Parting, he put his free hand to my shoulder. 'You look well.'

'Thank you.' I glanced down at his leg.

'Shrapnel and gangrene. It's a shame they don't make one-legged britches. They'd be half the price,' he joked, his lopsided grin briefly in evidence.

'We were told that you were dead.'

'They thought I was, but I'd been captured by the Union.'

'Fochik and Onsi?'

His expression dropped and he shook his head. 'Why did father tell me that you'd passed?'

'That is not a story for now. Have you the time to go somewhere and talk?'

Akocha nodded. 'Where shall we go?'

'Essy's,' I replied, knowing that she would still be stewing after the argument, but having no other choice.

He glanced at the ground with a puzzled expression. 'She knows you are alive and well?' he asked, looking back up at me.

'Yes. I visit with her regularly,' I stated, putting my arm through his while holding my hood in place with the other hand.

'Then why has she never said anything to me?' He continued to look perplexed as we set off.

'I will tell you when we get there,' I stated, beginning to worry that he would turn his back on me once in possession of the truth. 'How long have you been back?'

'I was released not long after the war ended,' he replied distractedly as he tried to unriddle the situation.

'That is nearly eight years ago.' I looked at him in surprise.

'I only ever visit the settlement with father when there are rations to be had at the Exchange,' he said. 'I should go and fetch him,' he added with sudden enthusiasm.

'No.' The word was stated forcefully and he looked at me questioningly.

'There is much you're not telling me.'

'I will tell all when we reach Essy's,' I replied. 'Do you remember when you used to carry me to the stream on your back?' I asked, hoping to change the topic of conversation.

Akocha turned his attention to the way ahead as we reached the alley that linked the two larger streets. 'I threw you in once,' he said, a smile of recollection dawning upon his face.

'You stood on the bank laughing as I stood chest deep and splashed water up at you. I remember thinking that the air seemed full of jewels.'

We fell into temporary silence as the memories came forth and we made our way to the far end of the alley. Reaching it, we crossed to the passageway alongside Essy's house.

Akocha stumbled, my eagerness to be hidden from sight unbalancing him.

'Sorry,' I said, noticing the silver crucifix about his neck which had been revealed by the disturbance.

He glanced at me and noted the direction of my gaze. Looking down, he took hold of the symbol of the Christ worshippers and tucked it back inside his pale shirt.

'You are a Christian?'

'I am. The path of Christ was revealed to me by a preacher as my health mended.'

'What of the Great Spirit?' I asked, recalling our conversations about the heritage of our people, Akocha having been determined that it should not be lost.

'There is a better path, one of forgiveness and love,' he replied.

'And all those times we spoke of the sacred traditions? Did your words mean nothing?' My tone became harder, his conversion sullying the past.

'I was young and ignorant of the glory of Our Saviour.'

'*Your* Saviour,' I corrected.

'Jesus is Our Saviour, whether or not you wish to believe it.'

We reached the door and I released the cloak in order to knock. It opened after a brief delay and Essy looked at us in shock.

'Nora! Peter!' she exclaimed, using his given name.

'May we come in?' I asked.

'Oh, yes of course,' she responded, stepping back and clearly flustered by our arrival.

We made out way in and I guided Akocha to the table as she shut the door behind us. Waiting until he was seated before withdrawing my arm, I looked to my sister.

'Why did you not tell me?'

'Father made me swear,' she replied without meeting my gaze, moving to the left side of the table where a half-stripped chicken carcass rested on a chopping board.

'You could have told me, no matter what Inki made you promise.'

'You still call him Inki?' commented Akocha.

'I still do and say a great many things that you once believed to be essential,' I said coldly, the deception of my sister and change in my brother serving to make me feel isolated and defensive.

'I swore a solemn oath that I would keep Peter's return a secret.'

'What is this all about?' he asked.

We both turned to him and my heart sank at the prospect of telling him the truth.

'Nora is an outcast,' blurted Essy before I had the chance to compose my response.

'An outcast?' He looked at me in confusion.

'Inki bought a slave,' I said, taking a deep breath. 'We fell in love and ran away from the farm.'

'You ran away with a nigger?'

I winced at his response. 'His name was Nicholas.'

'Was?'

'Inki shot him.'

Akocha was temporarily stunned by the revelations, staring at me in disbelief. 'I shouldn't be talking with you,' he stated solemnly, pushing up on the table and getting to his feet, 'and neither should you,' he added, looking to Essy.

'What?' It was my turn to show disbelief, astounded by his reaction.

'You broke the laws of the Nation. You knew them, you spoke of the traditions often, and therefore cannot plead innocence.'

'But you have turned your back on them.'

'I will not debate with you,' he responded as he passed me on the way to the door.

'And what of the forgiveness you spoke of outside?'

'I spoke of His forgiveness for our sins.' He stopped at the door, holding the handle.

'Is it a sin to love and to act out of that love?'

'I will have to tell father you've been allowing Nora to visit,' he stated, ignoring me and looking back at Essy.

'Please don't,' she pleaded, stepping towards him and clasping her hands together.

He considered a moment. 'Swear to me you will not let her visit again.'

'She'll do no such thing,' I said, stepping between them and glaring at him.

'I swear it.'

I glanced back at her in shock, overwhelmed by a feeling of betrayal.

'I will see you when Father and I return for supper,' said Akocha to our sister, opening the door and vacating the kitchen without glancing back.

The wind reached in and toyed with my hair as I faced the passageway. The contrast between my meeting with Hashi and what had just occurred served to magnify the pain of rejection.

In a rush of movement, I left the house, hurrying past Akocha as he hobbled along the passageway. Crossing the street beyond, I broke into a run, the hood down as I tried to escape the settlement as quickly as I could.

* * *

I spent the entire journey to the Olsens' seething with incredulity and bitterness, my stride quick and muscles filled with quivering tension. I could not believe Akocha's reaction to what I had done and his change of mind in regards our spiritual traditions. He had always known me to be a free spirit and strong-minded, and had once revelled in those traits, but now rejected me because of them. He spoke of love and forgiveness and yet displayed neither.

As for Essy, for her to cast me aside so easily was a thorn that sank deep beneath my skin. It irked me that our bond was so flimsy as to be undone by the mere threat of telling Inki. My visits were usually only twice a week and they were often foreshortened by circumstance, but they were valued, as was her continued contact despite the light in which I had been cast by following my heart.

The farm came into view across the grassland and I saw Marie hanging washing on the line to the left of the house, wearing a pale yellow housedress and white smock, the bandage still about her head. I made a beeline for her, needing comfort in my distressed state.

She looked over her shoulder at the sound of my approach, a cloth held to the line. Seeing the expression on my face, the wind wildly messing my hair, she lowered the chequered material.

'What's...?

I went to her and flung my arms about her before she could finish, holding her close.

She raised her arms and held me in turn as I buried my face at her neck and tried to stifle the sobs that immediately arose from deep within. My body shook as I fought to contain myself, a single tear passing down my cheek.

'Are you all right, Ishki?'

I quickly wiped away the tear before stepping from Marie. 'Just glad to be back,' I stated, turning to our son as he approached, Anders rounding the corner of the house behind him.

'Has the last calf been born yet?' I asked as Honung ran up to me and I fussed the hound briefly.

'Not yet. Uncle Anders thinks it will come this afternoon and if it doesn't we will help the cow give birth like we did before.'

He drew to a halt and I went to him, bending and giving him a hug. Seeing him left me in no doubt that leaving with you had been the right thing to do. He had issued from our love.

Stepping back, my expression saddened. His face... so like yours. The guilt in relation to my contact with Hashi arose once again, replacing the more recent feelings that had been ignited by the actions of my brother and sister.

Nicky cocked his head as he regarded me. 'What are you thinking about?' he asked as Anders stopped beside him and rested his hand on the boy's shoulder affectionately.

'How much you look like your father,' I replied.

'You're always saying that.'

'Because it is so apparent. You remind me of him every day.'

'I hope that's a good thing,' he said, having noted the change in my expression.

'It is,' I replied, bending and lifting him to me. 'You'll soon be too heavy,' I said as he draped his arms about my neck.

'Are you ready for lunch?' Marie asked Anders.

He nodded his response.

'I'll just finish hanging the washing. Fetch down some plates. The butter me and Nicky made is in the pantry and the bread in the oven should be ready,' she said.

Nicky's stomach groaned.

'Sounds like your stomach has good ears,' I joked.

'I'm starving,' he stated, pushing back on my arms to signal his wish to be put down.

I lowered him to his feet and he looked up at Marie as she turned to the line. 'Are there any oat cakes?'

'You ate the last of yesterday's and I haven't had the time to bake more,' she said over her shoulder, finally hanging the cloth she had been holding when I interrupted her and bending for the next item in the woven basket by her feet.

Nicky frowned, but made no complaint. 'I'm going to ride Rödbeta after we've eaten,' he said to me as Anders began towards the front door with Honung on his heels.

'What have you been doing this morning?' I asked as we followed.

'Me and Uncle Anders let the chickens out, collected the eggs and milked the cows. Then he went to check his traps while I stayed with Auntie Marie and made butter. When he got back we checked on the pregnant cow.'

'Sounds like you've been very busy,' I said as we went inside, allowing our son to enter first, the interior warmed by the stove and the smell of fresh bread hanging in the air.

'I hope he has not been too demanding,' I said to Anders, who had passed to the other side of the table and was taking plates down from the dresser.

'Not at all,' he said. 'It is our pleasure to have him here.' He placed them on the table and went into the pantry.

Returning with the covered butter dish, he put it down and went to the stove. Opening the door as Nicky's stomach grumbled again, he took a tea towel from the dresser and slid out the baking tin in which the new loaf rested, its crust golden.

'You should give your hands a wash,' I instructed, looking to our son as he rubbed Honung behind the ears and watched Anders put the steaming bread on top of the stove so the tin could cool.

He glanced round at me and then went to the bucket in the far corner, dipping his hands in and then reaching for the nearby cloth.

'Soap,' I stated, raising my eyebrow when he looked over at me.

He reluctantly picked up the pale bar from the floor beside and proceeded to clean his hands properly. The door opened and Marie entered with the empty basket, the wind almost pushing her in.

'The washing should dry quickly on such a day,' she said as she closed the portal and placed the basket beside.

Anders took his turn at the bucket after Nicky was done and we seated ourselves at our usual places, Marie taking the bread from the stove after checking the heat from the tin with a tentative touch. She placed it on the table and stepped to the dresser behind her chair. She took down the bread knife and returned, standing in order to slice the loaf.

'Smells good,' commented Nicky.

'Two herbs are mixed in. Can you guess what they are?' asked Marie as she began cutting.

Our son sniffed the air before shaking his head.

'I have put some basil in, along with…' She looked to Anders. 'Hur säger man vild vitlök?'

'Wild garlic,' he replied.

'Yes, wild garlic. It is good for the blood,' she stated. 'You will have to tell me what you think.' She handed him a plate with a couple of slices on.

Nicky reached for the butter, looking to the tabletop for a knife with which to spread it. 'Um…' He looked to Marie.

She glanced at Anders with a smile. 'You would be forgetting your own head if it weren't connected to your neck,' she said with amusement, quickly taking one from a drawer in the dresser and passing it to Nicky.

'Sorry,' said Anders with a twinkle in his eyes and smile upon his face.

I watched, feeling like an observer at a family meal once again, but this time finding no jealousy arising in response, the baby in Marie's belly having put pay to such foolishness. I could see how much they loved each other and they doted on Nicky because they loved him dearly too, but their love for their own child would be different, more profound. Their offspring would be of their blood, as Nicky was of ours.

'Chula?'

I looked to Marie, my gaze having settled on Nicky as the bread tore beneath the pressure of the hardened butter that he was attempting to spread. 'Thank you,' I said, taking the plate she was holding out to me.

Anders passed the butter once Nicky was finished and it was not long until we were all nearly ready to eat. I waited patiently with my hands upon my lap as Marie spread the last of her butter, not wishing to offend by starting before they said Grace and bracing myself for the sight of our son joining in. I recalled your lack of judgement and your own faith, one which I had never questioned, simply accepting you as you were.

They all bowed their heads.

'For what we are about to receive, may the Lord make us truly thankful,' said Marie.

'Amen,' they stated together.

I reached for my first slice, inhaling deeply as I raised it, my mouth watering in response to the scent of the herbs. Taking a large bite, I nodded and looked at Marie in appreciation.

'You like?'

'Very much,' I said through the food.

'You can watch me ride after we've eaten,' stated Nicky between mouthfuls.

I looked across at him and frowned. 'I can't stay, but will come back for you later.'

He looked surprised. 'Where are you going?'

'Home,' I replied. 'There are lots of chores to be seen to and I would like them done before you return so we can spend some time together without distraction,' I said, feeling a little guilty about concealing the fact I was meeting Hashi.

'Would you like my help? There's little for me to do here this afternoon,' said Marie.

'Thank you, but I will manage,' I said before taking another bite. 'What do you think of the bread?' I asked our son in an attempt to prevent any further discussion on the matter.

'It's delicious. Can you learn to make it like this?' he said, one side of his mouth bulging with food.

'You only have to add the herbs,' commented Marie. 'It's very easy.'

We ate the rest of our meal without speaking, savouring the flavour and freshness. I was lost to thought. So much had happened that morning and I was left with a strange sense of being dislocated from my life. The scene before me was a picture of normality, but most of what had preceded it was far from normal.

I shook my head, barely able to comprehend all that had come to pass in such as short space of time.

'Are you all right?'

I blinked and focussed on the bread in my hand. My thoughts had wandered while chewing on the previous bite and staring at what remained. I looked up at Marie. 'Fine,' I answered, forcing a smile of reassurance.

She regarded me doubtfully, but made no further comment as I placed the last of the bread into my mouth.

'Can I have another slice, thank you?' asked Nicky.

'Of course,' replied Marie, taking up the knife and cutting it. She put the slice on his plate and moved the butter close to him.

Anders leant back against his chair and stretched. Getting to his feet, he went around to the dresser and took down a cup. 'Have we any other water?' he asked after looking down at the nearby bucket, a few suds still in evidence after he and Nicky had washed their hands.

Marie glanced about the room. 'Where is the pail?'

'In the pantry. I haven't yet emptied the milk into the churn,' he replied.

'I'll empty it and visit the well when the meal is done. In the meantime, you could have some milk,' she suggested.

Anders went to the pantry and passed inside. Stepping back into view a few moments later, he stopped behind Nicky and lifted the cup to his lips, downing all the milk he had decanted into it and wiping his lips with the back of his hand.

'Would you like some?' asked Marie, turning to me.

'That would be good, thank you,' I responded.

'And you?' She looked to Nicky, who nodded as he chewed on his third slice.

'Three more cups of milk, thank you,' she stated, looking up at her husband with a smile.

Anders went back into the pantry and brought the pail out. Pouring three cups in turn, they were handed out and he returned to the confines of the small food store to decant the milk into the churn as we drank.

'We should go check on the expectant mother,' he said to Nicky when he reappeared, pail at his side ready to be rinsed and filled at their well.

Our son swallowed the last of his food and slipped from his chair with enthusiasm, a pale band of milk upon his upper lip.

'Come here,' I said, beckoning him over as Anders went to the door and Honung waited with tail wagging.

I wiped the residue away with my thumb and looked at his face a moment. Thinking about the coming meeting with Hashi, I bent and kissed his cheek. 'Have a good afternoon and be careful when you ride the horse.'

'I will,' he replied.

'I love you.'

'I love you too, Ishki.' He smiled and turned for the door, eagerly stepping over and putting on his boots.

Anders opened it and the hound went out into the overcast day. Nicky followed and Anders paused in the doorway.

'I love you too,' he said, looking to Marie and blowing a kiss.

She laughed and shooed him out with a wave of her hand, cheeks flushed.

The door shut and I began to rise in readiness to depart. Marie reached out and took my hand.

'I would speak with you,' she stated.

I settled back on the chair. 'Is there something wrong?'

'There's nothing wrong with me, but you were upset when you arrived and we did not get the chance to speak of it. What happened at the reservation?'

My expression fell as the morning's events came to the forefront of my mind. 'I had a row with Essy,' I stated. 'I will not be visiting again.'

'Over an argument?'

'There is more, but…' I took a deep breath. 'Can we speak of it another time?'

She looked into my eyes and nodded. 'If that is what you wish. We don't have to speak of it at all if you prefer, though sometimes it is better to let things out rather than hold them in.'

'I promise I will talk to you when I return.'

She continued to stare at my face. 'There is more to your wish to be home than you are saying,' she guessed.

'I am meeting someone,' I confirmed. 'I should go.'

She withdrew her hand from mine as I got to my feet.

'Thank you for the food and for looking after Nicky. You are good friends.'

'We are family,' she responded with a smile.

I returned the gesture, though it was tinged with sadness. Walking to the door, I took hold of the handle and opened it.

'Find the courage to love again,' she said as I was about to step out, apparently aware that I was going to meet a man, our previous conversation in regards love hinting at events in my life that had as yet gone unsaid.

I turned, finding her still looking at me, her eyes filled with affectionate concern.

'No love can last forever, Chula. The love you had with Nicholas would have come to an end one way or another. All things must pass, so do not fear to love again because of this.'

I stared at her a little longer and then nodded. 'Thank you,' I said before stepping out and closing the door.

* * *

Making my way home, I barely noticed the chill wind, my mind focussed inward. I thought on Marie's parting words. It was true that I feared feeling such pain and heartache as I had when you had been killed, but did not believe that was the reason for my growing doubt in regards a continuation of my contact with Hashi.

I still loved you and knew that love would endure until my last breath. How could I enter into another love when my heart already belonged to you? It felt like I was closing the door on the relationship I still maintained with you, not least through the visits to your grave.

I shook my head as the wind toyed with my hair, the hood of the cloak left down. I could not and would not bring an end to our bond.

Heading north up the vale, I felt increasingly tense at the thought of meeting with Hashi. I wished I had made no such arrangement and was tempted to turn and make my way back to the Olsens', only the thought that he would seek me out causing me to continue.

I passed the barn, feeling the presence of your grave despite the eastern wall hiding it from view. I wanted to visit with you, but was driven on by the wish to end my contact with Hashi as soon as possible.

The house came into view. He was already waiting, leaning on the boundary fence near the gate and yet to notice my approach. I braced myself for what had to be done, walking stiffly due to the tautness of my muscles.

Hashi looked over and the smile that at first arose soon faded when he noted my steely expression. 'It's good to see you, Chula,' he greeted, straightening. 'Is all well?'

I came to a stop at a distance. 'We cannot do this,' I stated, unable to look at him and instead staring at the grass between.

'What of this morning?' he asked in confusion.

'It was a mistake.'

'How can you say that?' he protested. 'I know you feel as I do.'

'You are wrong. My judgement was clouded by high emotion. Those clouds have cleared and I see the truth of it now.'

'No,' he said, shaking his head and taking a step forward, reaching out a hand. 'You have feelings for me.'

I took a step back, my eyes remaining guarded. 'I love Nicholas,' I stated.

'And I love both Jane and Oka,' he replied. 'We carry everyone we have loved in our hearts, but they all belong to the past.

'I am now,' he stated firmly, holding out his hand again, but without moving forward. 'Please, Chula, let go of your fear,' he said, echoing Marie's words.

'I am not afraid,' I responded, lifting my defiant gaze to his, but finding it faltering when confronted with the intensity of his eyes.

'You are afraid to open your heart for fear it will be broken again.' He looked to me imploringly. 'Take my hand and we can walk side by side through each new day.'

I shook my head and looked to the ground once more. 'No,' I said softly. 'To take hold of your hand I would have to release his.'

Hashi said nothing in response and I looked up again. He bore an expression of sad sympathy.

'You may hold his hand, but he does not hold yours,' he said regretfully, looking into my eyes briefly and then walking towards me.

I stepped away, but found him passing by. His head bowed, Hashi went south without a backward glance. I cannot deny that my heart ached at the sight as his parting words continued to echo about my mind.

I stood for long moments as he diminished. 'He does not hold yours,' I whispered, a shiver passing through me as realisation began to dawn, stirring deep within and building like steam in a kettle.

'You are gone,' I stated as if comprehending for the first time, my words taken on the wind as I felt your absence more keenly than ever before.

The pressure within grew.

I dropped to my knees and looked to the sky, thick cloud still hurrying south and Hashi no longer in sight.

Release came and I wept for yesterday, finally accepting that you were gone, my love.

* * *

I approached my brother's farm. The three eldest children were playing together in front of the house. The interaction was unusually harmonious as Celia and Helena turned the old cart wheel hanging from one of the only remaining trees, the rest having been cleared and used for fencing. The four ropes suspending the wheel twisted about each other as Simon sat in the middle, bracing himself for what was to come as his sister's giggled and the thud of a hammer arose from the western pasture to the right.

They released the wheel as I sought out my brother, seeing him at the far end of the field using a mallet to secure a new fence post, the bars to either side lying on the ground. Simon span wildly, gripping the old spokes as the ropes unwound and the girls stood back and watched in amusement.

I made for my brother, the coldness of Chula's reception having set a chill in me deeper than the wind could ever reach. I'd been foolishly hopeful after our meeting in the morning, one which had surpassed all expectations when she took my hand. Her warm hearted nature and the kiss born of it had sealed our connection, leaving me in no doubt that she was the woman I wanted to spend the rest of my life with.

The wheel turned the other way as I glanced back, the ropes creaking as Simon moved to grip the edge and vomited over the side, his sisters sent into fits of laughter.

'What have I told you before?' Emily appeared in the doorway with Elsa held to her, staring unhappily at her older children and the girls falling silent.

I raised my hand, but she gave no response.

'Come inside, all of you,' she instructed angrily.

I went to the near fence of the pasture and climbed over. Walking along a furrow in the planted field, I was careful not to tread on the seedlings, which were already a finger in height.

'Brother,' he nodded, testing the steadfastness of the post with a firm push and finding no movement.

'Is this the last to be done?'

'Yes,' he said, picking up the first of the fence bars by his feet and slotting it into a groove on the new post before aligning it with the one to the left.

I picked up the next and put it in place. 'Have you some spare time tomorrow?' I asked as he took the far end and secured it.

'That depends,' he said, taking the third from the ground and the two of us putting it up before stepping to the right and picking up the next length of fencing.

'I was hoping you'd help with something at my farm.'

He banged the length of timber into place with his fist and then looked to me as he straightened. 'You've been there?'

'I went this morning. There's much work to be done to make it habitable,' I stated, my parting words to Chula having made me realise that I was also clinging to the past.

'What do you need help with?' he asked, picking up the penultimate length.

'The rope…' I swallowed back, my stomach churning at the thought. 'The rope that Jane used may still be hanging in the pine wood.'

He stopped and looked over, his expression softening and eyes filled with pity. 'I'll come with you,' he confirmed. 'Do you intend to make it your home again?'

'I do.'

He nodded. 'I'm glad you've heeded my advice,' he said, turning his attention back to reconstructing the fence. 'You seemed set against moving back when we spoke before. What's changed your mind?'

'It's time to move on with my life,' I responded simply, taking up the last bar and the two of us fixing it in place. 'Most of the furniture has been taken,' I said as I dusted off my hands.

'You're lucky it's not worse. The house could have been used by those afflicted by alcohol or even burned to the ground,' he replied, taking the mallet from where it rested near the new post and then climbing the fence after testing it would take his weight.

He joined me at the edge of the field. 'The crops grow quickly, but it still isn't too late for you to plant your fields.'

'They will need clearing of weeds and ploughing first,' I responded as he began up a furrow and I took the one beside.

'You can use my ox and plough,' he offered.

'The two of us could see it done far more quickly than one.'

'With only one plough?'

'One could see to the weeds while the other ploughs.'

'As if I don't have enough to do here,' he said with a rye smile, glancing over at me. 'I will help you, Brother, but only this year so that you can be set to the task of living again.'

'Thank you.'

We reached the end of the field and climbed over. I began to make for the front door, but stopped when I found Duncan going towards the rear.

'Where are you going?'

'To put this in the barn,' he stated without turning, lifting the mallet.

I considered following him, but saw little point. Going to the door with a glance to the wheel the children had been playing on, I decided my first job at the farm would be to take down Oka's swing. With it gone and the knowledge that the rope had been removed from the trees at the rear of the property, maybe I could truly start to move on. Any other reminders had already been cleared from the house. The only thing left would be the location itself, and there was nothing I could do to change that other than create a new life there.

With a sigh, I opened the door and went inside, finding the children subdued as they sat on stools before the hearth. Simon still looked pale after his expulsion, one arm about his stomach and his head hanging low.

Emily turned from the stove. 'They are thinking on what they did,' she stated, giving them a hard look, her youngest seated next to her on the only seat with a back.

'They seemed to be getting on well,' I said, thinking it was a shame that they had been reprimanded for playing together, something that was increasingly rare as they became older.

'Making their brother sick is hardly what I'd call "getting on well",' she replied with continued irritation, turning back to the pot resting on the hotplate as Elsa spoke a few incomprehensible words, a little dribble snaking down her chin.

I made no further comment and went over to join the children. The sisters sat to the right of the fireplace and Simon to the left, so I moved a stool between and sat.

'How are you feeling?' I asked, looking at the boy's profile and feeling Emily's unkind gaze upon me. I expected to be admonished for speaking to him, but she remained silent, letting the noise of her agitated movements speak for her as she chopped vegetables for the broth.

'Still a bit sick,' he said with a glance at his mother over my shoulder. 'We shouldn't be speaking,' he added in a whisper.

'I thought it looked like fun,' I replied, Simon glancing sideways at me with a smile upon his face.

* * *

'What is it?' Marie studied my expression, immediately detecting that something had changed as I approached.

'I have let go of his hand,' I replied somewhat cryptically as I joined her in the doorway to the barn, the new calf trying to get to its feet in the large stall at the rear.

She looked into my eyes. 'Truly?' she asked, apparently understanding what I meant.

'Truly.'

She smiled and her eyes sparkled with tears as she stepped forward and took me into a warm embrace. 'I have waited for this time,' she stated, 'but didn't think it would be so long to come.'

'You have been waiting?' I asked after we parted.

'You have been holding on to Nicholas for a great many years. For us that has been clear, but for you...' She shook her head. 'You could not see it and it would have mattered little what we said to you.'

She rested her hand upon my shoulder. 'Was it the new man that opened your eyes?'

I looked down. 'In a way, yes.'

'In a way?' She ducked to look up my face. 'What do you mean?'

'I told him that I want nothing to do with him and his parting words cut right to the truth of my life.' I took a breath. 'I did not see it until it was too late.'

'I don't think you'd pick a hard hearted man, so surely he will understand.'

'I was cruel.'

'You?' she said in surprise as Anders and Nicky spoke to each other, the former leaning against the wall of the stall while my son sat atop, still watching the newborn and both with their backs to us as Honung rested at her master's feet.

'This morning...' I looked up at her. 'This morning I kissed him. Then, this afternoon, I rejected him with such cold certainty that I would not blame him if he took to hating me.'

'No one could hate you, Chula.' She lifted her hand from my shoulder and stroked my cheek briefly. 'You are one of the dearest people I've ever met.'

'You did not feel what was between us when I visited his farm nor see how poorly I treated him at mine. He would have to be very forgiving.'

'And is he?'

I shrugged.

'Then I suggest you find out,' she said as Anders lifted Nicky down and they began to wander over,

Honung raising her head and watching a moment before deciding to follow.

'How can I face him after what I did?'

'Find a way,' she said softly, keeping her voice low so the men would not hear. 'A fine new cow,' she stated, turning to her husband.

'And one to add to the herd or sell at market,' he smiled, the calf female.

'You missed us pulling it out again,' said Nicky as he stopped before me. 'You also missed me riding, but Anders says I can ride Rödbeta again to show you.'

'Why not give her a rest and show me tomorrow?'

'Are we visiting again?'

'I thought you may like to stay one more night,' I replied, turning to Marie and Anders. 'If you don't mind.'

'Not at all,' replied Marie, realising that I must be thinking of visiting with Hashi to try and mend what I had done.

'There,' I said, looking back at my son. 'Would you like to stay?'

Nicky nodded enthusiastically.

'Then you can show me your riding skills when I come for lunch.'

'Can you bake some more oat cakes?' He looked up at Marie.

'Always the oat cakes,' she said with a chuckle. 'Of course.'

'Has Auntie Esther made anymore of her strawberry sponge yet?' he asked, once more focussing his attention on me.

'I do not think she will be making them again,' I replied, my expression falling as I was reminded of what had happened earlier.

'Why not?'

'Let's go inside,' said Marie, seeing my discomfort.

'We must see to feeding and watering the calves and their mothers,' said Anders, glancing over his shoulder. 'They are also in need of straw. I think it's going to be a cold night.' He looked out of the doors.

I turned and saw that the thick cloud was clearing from the north.

'You'll need to be bringing in more firewood,' said Marie. 'We'll have the stove and fire to keep going.'

Anders gave a nod. 'Do you want to help me?' he asked, looking to my son.

'What do you want me to do?'

'I think we'll see to their food first,' replied the Swede. 'Do you think you can carry a sack all by yourself?'

'I can try,' said Nicky, going to the sacks piled to the left.

We all watched with amusement as he tried to lift one, its size nearly equal to his own and the outcome a forgone conclusion. Nicky grinned at us and was undeterred. Holding on to the top corners, he gritted his teeth and his face became flushed with effort. He staggered forward a little with the weight of the sack and nearly fell face first as it began to tip.

Anders quickly rushed to his aid, righting the sack and taking hold of my son to make sure he did not tumble. 'That was close,' he said, giving Nicky's arm a squeeze.

* * *

'When will you go and see him?' enquired Marie as I took four bowls from the dresser and she looked into the oven to check on the pie.

'In the morning,' I replied, placing them on the stove in readiness for when she served the food. 'I thought it wise to let a little time pass after what I said to him this afternoon.'

She closed the door and straightened. 'It's nearly done.'

I pulled out the seat at the far end that Nicky usually occupied and sat with my back to the wall. 'In truth, I am not sure how to find him. I could go ask my sister, but…' I let the sentence go unfinished.

'Doesn't he live at his farm?' Marie stood by the stove, savouring its heat as the temperature dropped due to the clearing cloud.

I shook my head. 'He experienced loss greater than mine and it has kept him from his home.'

Her expression became thoughtful as she tried to work out how to locate him. 'I could come with you and ask about the town,' she suggested, brightening as the idea came to her.

'You would do that?'

'For you,' she replied, nodding. 'We will go first thing in the morning. I will come to yours so that Nicky does not ask questions.'

'What will you tell Anders?'

'The truth. He will be as happy as I that you are releasing the past and looking to the present,' she said. 'But you must tell me one thing first.'

'What?'

'His name,' she smiled.

I couldn't help but laugh. 'His name is Hashi. It means 'Moon' in Chickasaw.'

'A fine name,' she said, nodding again. 'The moon watches over the fox and lights its way as it moves through the night.'

I looked at her with affection as the front door opened and Honung padded in ahead of Nicky and Anders.

'The food is nearly ready,' announced Marie as they took off their boots.

* * *

I reached the house at dusk. Quickly feeding the chickens, I shut the coop and made my way to the gate. As I walked along the path, I noticed weeds thickening the herb and vegetable beds. With so much time spent away, there was an increasing amount of work to be done and I thought about setting to clearing the unwanted plants then and there.

The cold caused me to continue to the door and I entered the darkness that waited. Leaving the shutters open on what little light remained of the day, I hastened to the hearth and readied a fire.

The match flared as I struck it on the floorboards and placed it to the kindling, the flame taking but without vigour as the chill pushed in. It faded and died as I knelt before it, the twigs and hay having become a little damp with the absence of activity within the house.

Trying again, I met with an equal lack of success. Glancing over my shoulder, my gaze settled on the lamp resting on the sideboard to the rear of the room.

Fetching it, I carefully poured a little of the oil onto the kindling. I struck a third match and leant back, narrowing my eyes against the expected onrush of flame as I dropped it onto the waiting combustibles.

The fire burst into life, its flare of sudden heat upon my face as I moved further back and selected some small logs from the pile beside the chimneybreast. Placing them on and being careful not to extinguish the flames, I got to my feet and went to the window to close the shutters.

A dark figure was moving purposefully along the boundary fence towards the gate, a crutch used in lieu of a missing leg.

'Akocha!' I exclaimed, my pulse quickening.

He entered the garden and began up the path without pause. I looked to the door, expecting a knock.

It was flung open, banging against the wall as Akocha walked in, the end of the crutch thumping against the boards. He came to a halt and scanned the room, eyes settling on me as I stood in shock.

'Where is he?' he demanded, expression stern and unkind.

'Who?' I asked, my voice barely a whisper in the wake of his abrupt arrival.

'Father,' he replied.

I looked at him in confusion. 'Inki?'

'Where is he, Nora?' he reiterated, taking a threatening step forward.

'I have not seen him in years.'

'Just tell me where he is.'

'I do not know.'

'Liar!' He snapped, taking another step closer and raising his fist. 'I saw him coming this way at sundown,' he seethed, 'and it's not the first time.'

'I do not know what you are talking about,' I replied, eyes widened by fear.

'I thought nothing of his wanderings until this day,' he said, shaking his head and looking upon me with disgust. 'What did you say to make him visit with you? Did you wring out his heart with your treacherous ways? Haven't you already done enough to bring about his ruin?'

'I have done nothing.'

'You left and Mother died because of it,' he replied, his body quaking with fury. 'You betrayed our family and our people. You are an accursed creature,' he hissed, spittle spraying from his lips. 'Tell me where Father is or…'

My gaze moved beyond Akocha as another figure stepped through the open door.

'I am here.'

My brother was given a start by the deep voice as I stared at Inki. He was stooped with age and it was then that I knew for certain it had been him in the woods and at the gate.

'Leave your sister be,' he instructed.

'But…'

'Leave your sister be,' he repeated, his weathered face lit by the firelight.

Akocha hesitated and then stepped back, turning to face our father. 'What are you doing here?'

Inki did not answer. I stared at him, recalling his silhouette in the doorway to mine and Essy's room. Dread and distaste reared their heads despite all the years that had passed since I had last endured a visitation.

'You must ignore whatever it is she has said to bring you here. She is an outcast and we should have nothing to do with her.'

'She said nothing. I came of my own free will,' he stated, taking his gaze from me and looking to his only remaining son. 'Wait for me at the gate.'

'You must come with me,' said Akocha.

'At the gate,' he said firmly.

My brother looked at me over his shoulder, his eyes filled with disdain. Making his way towards the door, Inki stepped aside to allow him to pass, the thump of the crutch marking his progress. He walked out and was temporarily hidden from sight, coming into view again through the window as he made his way along the path.

'This is the only time I will speak with you,' began Inki.

'It was you at the gate,' I stated.

He nodded slowly. 'I've been in the valley a number of times.'

'Why?'

'For this. I hadn't the will to put voice to words before tonight, but your brother's actions created the need.'

'You killed Nicholas,' I said, finding it hard to hate the man before me, age having reduced him in stature, though strength remained in his gaze.

'I did not come to talk of the past.'

'Then what do you want?'

'I feel the shadow of death deepening at my back. It won't be long before it overtakes me and I go to join our ancestors.' He shifted with discomfort, wincing as he did so. 'You have a fine son.'

'Who is without a father.'

Inki sighed. 'This is how I thought it would be,' he stated. 'You have my stubbornness and fight.'

'You can hardly expect me to welcome you with open arms after what you visited upon me and upon Nicholas.'

'I will go.' He turned and moved towards the door.

'Wait,' I called, stepping forward. 'Make your peace, such as it is,' I said, understanding that the words he wished to say were intended to help him face death and accept it with nothing left undone, my compassion overriding the other feelings that his presence gave rise to.

'I saw a man here yesterday,' he stated, turning back to me.

I nodded. 'He was checking to see if the property had been abandoned,' I lied, not wishing Hashi to be deemed an outcast for knowingly having contact with me, especially as our potential union may have been undone by my hurtful words.

Inki stared into my eyes, seeing the deception. 'Take a husband. Give my only grandchild a father and bring him up in the ways of our people.'

I bit back my immediate and heated response. 'Nicholas,' I said instead. 'Your grandson's name is Nicholas, after his father.'

'I did not come to seek your forgiveness and you should not seek mine,' he said in response to my accusatory tone.

'Your forgiveness?

His face tightened and his eyes narrowed. 'If you hadn't run away with that ni…' He stopped himself, taking a calming breath. 'If you hadn't left with the slave, then your mother may have lived to see the return of her son, which in turn may have brought her back to us.'

I stared at him, unable to find the words with which to reply. Until my brother's accusation concerning Ishki, I had not given her passing much thought other than to mourn. 'Her passing was not my fault,' I stated.

'The break you caused was the last her heart could take,' said Inki, sadness causing his expression to fall as he glanced down at the boards.

'I did not intend it to be that way,' I responded.

'I have said all I want to say,' he announced after a moment's pause. 'We will not meet again.'

'I…' The words stuck in my throat. 'I forgive you,' I stated, Hashi's parting comment that afternoon having released me from the past and allowing my forgiveness of what had transpired.

Inki looked at me, studying my expression and finding no lie. He gave a nod and then went to the door. Taking hold of the handle, he closed it without another glance.

I looked to the view out of the window, watching his bent form make its way to where Akocha waited at the gate. They moved away in the deepening darkness, my brother putting his arm about the old man, who offered no protest as they were consumed by the night.

I glanced at my shadowy reflection as I was overcome by shaking in the wake of the visit. Neglecting to close the shutters, I moved on unsteady legs to the chair before the fire. Sitting, I rested back and tried to calm myself. The muscles in my neck were filled with tension and I rolled my head on my shoulders in an attempt to relieve it.

I yawned and stretched, the events of the day taking their toll. My thoughts were sluggish as I reached forward and placed new logs on the fire, grateful for the heat as I remained in my cloak.

Moving the chair closer, I reclined once again. Letting my mind drift, I felt the tension sink out of me and succumbed to sleep.

* * *

I sat alone before the dying embers. Chula occupied my thoughts as I recollected the two meetings we'd had that day. The first had been filled with hope, hope that had been quashed so thoroughly by her coldness in the afternoon. I wondered what had happened to cause such a change, considered the possibility that someone had spoken to her about me and mentioned my recent past as a drunkard. It seemed unlikely considering her status and I cast the idea aside.

Shaking my head, I was unable to fathom what could have brought about such distance, nor could I fathom any way to close it. She'd made it abundantly clear that I was not to approach her again and I wouldn't go against her wishes.

'Maybe she is something more I must let go of,' I mumbled to myself, one of the embers cracking as it cooled.

My mind turned to what was ahead instead of what was behind. The visit to the farm the following morning loomed large and cast a long shadow. I had no inclination to go in truth, but knew the goodwill of Emily was wearing thin and my time at my brother's was necessarily limited by the forthcoming addition to the family. There was little choice but to try and live with the memories that resided in the house that had once been home to my family.

I shivered at the prospect of spending even one night there. The ghosts of my past were sure to stir and I feared a return to the bottle in order to find both sleep and escape. There were still occasions when I heard the call of the alcohol, but alone out there, it was sure to come loud and often.

The gentle and regular tap of wood against wood arose from along the hall and I knew that my brother and Emily were being intimate. Not wishing to listen to the rhythm of their love making, I rose from the stool and went to the door, taking down my coat and hat. Putting them on and then slipping on my boots without doing up the laces, I stepped out and was embraced by the deep cold.

Walking over to the old cart wheel, I sat on its edge, the ropes creaking as it swayed a little. I placed my feet on the ground to still it and then lay back, spying the full moon between the branches above, which were still now that the wind had ceased.

'Chula,' I breathed, the mist of her name hanging in the air before me, ungraspable and fleeting.

* * *

I woke with a start and stared at the last of the flames in the fireplace. They licked from between the black remains of logs like tongues tasting the night. In the dream I had come around the corner of the house to find Nicholas, not Inki, at the front gate.

My heart was still pounding and I took a few moments to calm myself, still wearing the dress I so despised and the cloak over it. The front of the latter had come open and I could feel the chill upon my chest as I drew it tight and held it in place.

Sitting up, I selected slender branches and placed them on the fire, hearing a slight hiss as the dampness within them was exorcised by the heat. Watching until satisfied that the flames would become stronger. I glanced over my shoulder, feeling hungry and wondering if I should have some food.

Noting pale light upon the window frame, I got to my feet and went to look out at the moon, discovering she was in her fullness.

'Hashi,' I whispered, my breath upon the glass.

I was overcome by the urge to visit your grave. My cloak and boots still on, I followed the impulse and went to the door, glancing back when the fire spat. Seeing that no embers had been thrown out, I exited the house and went along the path to speak with you one last time.

I passed through the gate, the landscape made dreamlike by the pale coating of moonlight. Going right, I made my way past the young trees. Walking by the western wall of the barn, I looked in through the tumbledown gap and saw the soft shapes of the stones that covered your resting place.

Entering, I passed along the short trail through the undergrowth and stepped over the recent spill of stones. Reaching the graveside, I knelt on the damp ground, feeling the moisture seep into the cloak and dress as I rested my hand on the top stone.

'Nicholas,' I stated in the hush, trying to compose the right words. 'You were the sun in my sky, my love, but in the night that has come since your passing, a moon has risen.' My breath hung pale over the grave, as if your spirit were rising from the stones.

'I will always love you, but our time together has long been over. I have lived in denial for too long, have tried to hold onto you, never seeing that you no longer held onto me,' I stated, my words echoing those spoken by Hashi.

'I will leave you to rest as you must leave me to live.' Tears glittered in my eyes. 'I will not come again.'

I hesitantly removed my hand and got to my feet, tears beginning to fall. 'Chi-hollo-li,' I whispered in parting, longing to hear your voice reply in kind, but only the screech of an owl answering.

Walking away, the moonlight was captured in my tears as they fell to the grass. 'Goodbye, Nicholas.'

Saturday, April 12, 1873

I sat with a cup of coffee cradled in my hands, the warmth barely penetrating as the steam rose into the coldness. The fire had gone out during the early hours, but I did not have the will to relight it, especially with Marie due early.

I wanted to change out of the white folk's dress and into my buckskin, but the knowledge that I would have to visit the settlement kept me seated. Instead, I tried to focus on what I was going to say to Hashi by way of apology. No clear approach made itself apparent, partly due to the tired fog that had yet to lift from my mind.

The thought of visiting Nicholas' grave came to mind. It was dismissed, only to re-emerge a little later. After years of going to the ruin every morning, the idea derived as much from habit as the wish to commune with him.

'You are not communing with him, only the thought of him,' I said to the silence of the room.

Turning my gaze to the window, I saw the top of the eastern hill edged in gold as the sun rose beyond. I longed for its touch and decided to take a walk in the vale.

Drinking the coffee in quick gulps, knowing that time was limited and I would have to keep the house in sight just in case Marie arrived before I was back, I then rose and went to the table. Placing the cup on the top, I went to the door and passed outside.

The temperature inside the house had dropped after the fire had gone out and I found little difference in the open air as I walked to the gate. Passing out of the garden, I made left and followed the boundary fence around to the chicken coop and neighbouring shed where the feed was kept.

Opening the coop to the gentle clucks of its inhabitants, I moved towards the western hill behind the house. I passed through sparse trees, reaching its foot and making my way up.

Setting my sights on the bright crest of the hill before me, I saw a buzzard sitting on a small outcrop. Wary of my proximity, it took to the sky, flying in the opposite direction. I watched it ascend, keeping low over the slope as it climbed with grace. It passed into the sunlight, glowing and golden, a phoenix reborn out of the shadows.

I smiled as my calves strained with the exertion and I pushed on at a pace, the vale still holding the night's chill and my misty breath trailing behind. Looking back from time to time, I saw no sign of Marie, the house increasingly distant.

I slowed as I neared the threshold where shadow gave way to light. Taking a breath as if about to dive into water, I walked forward, feeling the tender warmth of the springtime sun upon the back of my head.

I turned when I was fully immersed in the light. Closing my eyes to the glare, I opened my arms wide, seeing the buzzard in my mind's eye and imagining myself taking flight, as I had often done as a girl.

I was golden. I was reborn.

* * *

'Hejsan,' greeted Marie.

I looked up as I knelt by one of the vegetable patches, the weeds in my hands being added to the pile beside me. 'Hej,' I replied, wiping my hands together to remove excess dirt as I got to my feet.

She walked up to the gate and entered the garden. 'Do you want to be going straight away?'

'I just need to wash my hands,' I replied, glancing to the rear of the house and seeing that the sun was now catching the top of the trees at the base of the hill.

'Something has changed,' she observed. 'You seem... lighter?'

'I have changed,' I smiled.

She looked at me curiously.

'A continuation of letting go,' I responded to her silent enquiry.

Maria gave a nod.

I walked towards the house, my fingers numbed by the cold and breath still lingering in the air.

Going inside and leaving the door open, I went to the bucket of water on the far side of the table and quickly washed off the smears of mud. Drying my hands, I hid them inside my sleeves and hoped they would soon regain some warmth.

'I think the cold spell Anders spoke of is already coming to an end,' stated Marie as I reappeared, closing the door behind me and making my way to her as she remained just inside the gate.

'I hope so,' I replied, reaching her and the Swede leading us out of the garden. 'My fingers are frozen.'

We turned right and headed south. When the barn came into view, I noticed that a section of the northern wall had collapsed inward, a couple of stray stones having fallen on the nearside.

'How is Nicky this morning?'

'Excited to show you how well he rides Rödbeta,' she replied, 'and to have oat cakes when I return and bake them for him,' she added, glancing at me with a grin upon her gentle face.

I laughed. 'He certainly enjoys your baking, and the company of both you and Anders.'

I reached out and took hold of her arm, bringing her to a halt. 'Thank you both for everything you have done for us,' I stated. 'You are beloved friends.'

'As you are to us,' she responded.

I smiled and took her into my arms, giving the Swede a brief hug and blinking tears from my eyes.

We set off again, staying silent until we reached the southern end of the vale and walked into the sunlight.

'What will you say to him?' asked Marie.

'I do not know,' I admitted. 'I have tried to think of the right words, but they will not come.'

'They will come when needed,' she assured me.

'I hope you are right.'

'Just speak from your heart and you will be fine. It is a good heart, Chula, and I'm certain he sees that.'

I made no reply, my thoughts turning to the meeting with Hashi that I hoped would come of the journey to the settlement. There was no guarantee that we would discover his location and even if we did, it may be that approaching him would be impossible if others were present. I had no wish for him to be tarred with the same brush as I, not by my doing. If he chose to forgive my coldness and accepted the consequences of a union with me, then that was fine, but I would not foist such a position upon him.

'Do not worry,' stated Marie. 'He will accept your apology.'

I turned to find her looking at me. 'Do you think we will find him?'

'I've no doubt,' she replied.

'Then you have more confidence than me.'

We walked through the brush towards the main track into the settlement, passing small woods and thickets of tight bushes. The grass sighed against our clothes as birds sang. The heat of the sun was not as strong as it had been before the cold snap, but was still a welcome touch upon my cheeks as I felt a nervous lightness in my stomach in anticipation of seeing Hashi again.

* * *

I walked up the hall towards the main room, hearing a shriek from one of the girls. Simon suddenly appeared in the entrance before me and sprinted by, quickly diving into his room.

'Come back and apologise,' shouted Helena as she stepped into sight, hands on hips.

I passed her and found Emily comforting Celia before the fire. She was crying as Elsa stood unsteadily before her, the youngster holding onto one of her knees for support and looking up at her enquiringly.

'What happened?' I asked her older sister.

'Simon put a spider down her dress,' she replied with disapproval.

I tried not to smile, but she noted the amusement in my eyes and gave a shake of her head before turning away and going to her sister's side.

'Always acting up,' said Duncan as he sat at the kitchen table on the left, a cup of warm milk before him, as was his habit after breaking the fast.

I took the seat opposite him after glancing out of the window, seeing that it was a fine day. 'Are you still happy to come to the farm?'

He nodded, his elbows resting on the table as he raised the cup and took a sip, his eyes temporarily closing.

'You need to speak to your son,' stated Emily, picking up Elsa and holding her to her chest before coming over to the table, Helena remaining by Celia's side and assuring her that the spider was gone.

'Can't it wait? He was only fooling around.'

'No, it can't,' she replied sternly.

He took a deep breath as he set the cup on the table. Rising, he gave me a look which summed up his embattled state. 'They've been at it all morning so far,' he said as he made for the hall.

'Maybe they should extend school to seven days a week,' I joked, attempting to lighten his mood.

'That's not a bad idea,' he replied before disappearing from sight.

Emily watched her husband pass into Simon's room and then turned her attention to me as her youngest played with her hair. 'Duncan tells me you're both going to your farm. He says you'll be moving back there as soon as you're able.'

I nodded.

'I'm glad.'

I looked up at her, eyebrows rising slightly.

'I didn't mean that I'm glad you'll be leaving,' she added quickly, cheeks flushed. 'Only that I'm glad you're returning to your life.'

'I know,' I responded, fully aware that she'd be relieved to see the back of me.

'Would you like some warm milk?' she asked, still a little flustered and stepping towards the stove.

'I'm fine, thank you.'

'There,' said Duncan as he returned. 'All done.'

'What's his punishment?' asked Emily as he went to retake his seat.

'I gave him a scolding, isn't that enough?'

She looked at him, her expression clearly portraying her belief that he hadn't done what was expected. 'I'll go and deal with it, shall I?' she asked rhetorically, sighing with exaggeration and walking to the hall, Elsa still in her arms.

'Shall we go?'

'You don't want to wait until Emily comes back?'

Duncan frowned. 'I think she'd probably prefer to find me gone. The children are supposed to be helping her with the chores around the house and so I'm not needed.'

I got up from my seat and we made our way to the door. Donning my coat and hat, I briefly bent to put on my boots. Doing up the laces, I straightened and took hold of the handle.

'See you both later,' I said in parting to Celia and Helena, neither turning to me as the latter sat on a stool with an arm about her younger sister's shoulder.

'Your uncle just spoke to you,' stated Duncan.

'Bye,' said Helena with a touch of sarcasm that wasn't lost on my brother, his eyes narrowing as he regarded his eldest and considered reprimanding her.

I placed my hand on his forearm. 'Come,' I stated, opening the door.

We left the house. The brightness and open space were a welcome relief after the confines of the dingy interior, which always felt so crowded when the entire family were in the main room, especially if the atmosphere were soured by misbehaviour.

Taking a deep breath, I set off with Duncan beside me. We followed the path to the main track into town, turning west as Chula came to mind. I pushed the thoughts aside, attempting to release her as I was attempting to release my past.

* * *

We came out of the brush and onto the track, making right. Two men were walking in the same direction a hundred yards ahead and I narrowed my eyes as I looked at them.

'Hashi,' I breathed, recognising the coat and hat.

Marie turned to me. 'He is one of them?' she asked, keeping her voice lowered.

'Yes,' I replied with a nod.

'Which one?'

'On the left.'

'Then it seems fate has been kind and you have found him already,' she said with a smile. 'Will you call his name?'

I shook my head. 'If he is seen with me…'

'Then what do we do?'

'I will follow,' I replied, slowing and bringing us to a halt. 'There is no need for you to stay now that he has been located.'

'I don't mind remaining, if that is your wish.'

'No, but thank you,' I said, shaking my head. 'Nicky will be happy to have you back and to help make the oat cakes,' I added with a thin smile.

Marie nodded, glancing along the track at the men who were receding from sight. 'You had better get after them,' she said.

I stepped forward and embraced her. 'Thank you, Marie.'

'I did nothing,' she replied as we separated.

'I will see you for lunch.' I set off again.

'Good luck,' she said in parting.

I set my gaze on the backs of the two men and increased my pace until I was within fifty yards of them, careful to walk with as little noise as possible. Pulling my hood up as the settlement drew into sight, I felt nervous as I considered offering Hashi my apologies.

Passing between the first buildings, I kept my head low, only just able to see the two men's boots as they continued up the main street. They neared the Exchange and I expected them to join the queue that was already forming in readiness to receive rations, but they passed it by.

I raised my head a little, glancing around to see if Inki or Akocha were present, but neither of them apparent.

Hashi veered to the left and entered the hardware store, the other man remaining outside. I moved to the entrance of the street that ran beside the Exchange and tried to look inconspicuous, catching a glimpse of the man's face and realising they must be related, such was the similarity.

Hashi reappeared carrying a broom, which he placed over his shoulder as he rejoined the other man and they continued westward. I stepped out of the side street and followed, soon reaching the outskirts of the town.

'His farm,' I stated in realisation as a cart rolled by in the other direction and I passed the rundown shack where I knew an old medicine man to live.

I felt more at ease as I left the settlement behind, lagging back to increase the distance and decrease the chance of discovery. I moved into the trees to the right, weaving through them and catching glimpses of the men ahead.

They made their way onto the second track heading north and I watched from behind a trunk, seeing Hashi glance back. I smiled sadly at the sight of his face, the lightness in my stomach increasing.

I lingered in the trees awhile after they had passed from view. Feeling claustrophobic within the confines of the hood, I pulled it down. Taking settling breaths, their mist hung before me and was lit by rays of sunlight slanting through the leafy branches.

Rolling my head on my shoulders, my tension building, I exited the wood and made for the path that would take me to him. Taking the turn, I found no sign of them ahead, only their footprints guiding me onward.

Reaching the bend about the rocky outcrop, I moved close to its concealment and stared along the track. The house rested ahead, but neither of the men were in view. If I approached directly there was every chance of being seen and so I chose to move into the bushes and undergrowth.

Sneaking through and keeping low, I kept my gaze firmly fixed on the rundown dwelling. The darkness of the open doorway gave no hint of anyone inside and there were no sounds to provide me with a clue as to Hashi's location.

Arriving at the boundary fence, I crouched in the tall grass. Brushing an insect from my cheek, I watched and listened.

The man who had been accompanying Hashi came into view around the right-hand side of the house, a coiled length of old rope in hand. My pulse increased when I saw the noose at its end, realising what its sorry use had been.

He paused at the corner of the building, glancing at the doorway before undoing the hoop. The task done, he went to the entrance and dropped the rope beside before entering.

I could hear mumbled voices and strained to hear what was being said, the words escaping me. Waiting, neither man made an appearance.

I slipped between the bars of the fence, my heart pounding as I moved into plain sight. Bent over and fleet of foot, I quickly made my way to the wall slats, reaching them without discovery and flattening myself against them. I could hear sweeping in the main room and wondered which of the men was set to the task.

Moving carefully along the wall, I crouched as I drew close to the entrance. Peering around the post, I spied Hashi brushing leaves from the far corner.

Sidling forward so I could see the rest of the room, I found no trace of the other man. Gathering myself with a breath, I straightened and stepped into view.

'Hashi?'

* * *

The whisper of my name caused me to turn. Chula stood in the doorway and my pulse raced at the sight of her silhouetted against the brightness of the day.

She took a step and her features became clearer as she entered. 'I am sorry,' she said softly.

My heart melted like ice beneath the warmth of the sun at the sound of her words.

'What you said…,' she began, glancing at the dusty floor as she tried to find words. 'You were right.'

I was about to move towards her when hammering sounded from the back room. She looked to the corridor in startled alarm.

'It's just my brother securing sidings that have rotted and slipped out of place,' I reassured.

'You are moving back?'

'I had thought to,' I replied, wishing to take her into my arms, but the intrusion of the blunt noise keeping us apart.

'Then I am too late?' she looked into my eyes, a blush upon her cheeks.

'Too late?'

'I sought to mend the break and discover what we might have together.'

The hammering ceased as I stared at her, palms becoming clammy against the handle of the broom. 'You would have me?'

'I would,' she nodded. 'If you still wish to have me.' Chula held my gaze, searching my eyes.

I released the broom and went to her, stopping short of taking her into my arms. 'There is nothing I want more.'

'What are you doing?'

My brother's horrified words caused us both to turn.

'Isn't she the outcast?' he asked, stopping in the entrance to the main room.

'She is,' I stated, Chula stepping away from me.

'Then you should have nothing to do with her.'

'I'll do as I wish with my life.'

'Even throw it away?' he asked.

I reached for her hand, taking it despite her hesitation to take hold. 'I would not be throwing it away, I'd be living it with the woman I love,' I stated.

Chula turned to me in surprise. 'You think you love me?'

'I do not think it, I know it,' I stated, holding her gaze. 'I knew it from the first moment I saw your face.'

'Listen to yourself,' scoffed Duncan. 'How can you love someone you barely know? It's ridiculous.'

'Then I am ridiculous,' I retorted, returning my attention to him. 'There are many kinds of love and many ways it finds its way into people's hearts. I had no idea you knew them all.'

Duncan shook his head and snorted. 'If one of the children said such a thing I'd scold them for being foolish.'

'But I am not a child, Brother, and I know my own heart better than anyone who would judge from a distance.'

'I say your mind has been addled by the drink.'

'And yours by the opinions of others and your own limited experience,' I responded with growing heat to my words.

He stared at me a moment, considering his next words. 'If you don't send her away, then I will go,' he stated, 'and you are never to return to my home.'

'Then go, Brother,' I replied without hesitation.

He looked to Chula with distaste before returning his gaze to me and shaking his head once again. Without another word, he trooped across the room, brushing past me and exiting the house.

We watched him march away along the track, a hush left in his wake as the birds sang in the sunlight. I felt no loss, only her closeness and the contact of her hand, knowing that I had made the right decision.

* * *

Hashi's brother vanished from sight around the outcrop. I could feel him next to me, more real than ever before. Thanks to his words, I had come to accept the possibility of our union and with that acceptance he was made more substantial. Without guilt or a feeling of betrayal keeping him at bay, I had allowed him in.

'You should run and catch up with him or you will be made an outcast like me,' I said, still concerned that I would not be all he hoped me to be.

'I've made my choice,' he replied, turning to me and squeezing my hand. 'We'll be outcasts together.'

He bent forward and placed his lips to mine. Our eyes open, I was lost to the depths of his gaze.

'Your words about love,' I began when the kiss came to an end, 'are you certain?'

'I'm certain,' he said, gaze unwavering.

I stared at him as his words sank in. 'What now?' I asked.

'Will you take a man who has nothing but the clothes he's wearing?' he said with a glance down at himself.

'I do not judge a man on what he has, but what he is,' I replied, smiling softly.

'Then I hope you judge me to be worthy of your affection.'

'There is nothing to make me doubt it.' I went on tiptoes and kissed him, intending it to be a brief caress, but finding his arms about me as he held me close and long.

I looked out of the door thoughtfully when we parted. 'If you are to be regarded as an outcast, you will have no place on the reservation,' I stated. 'You will have to take Nicky's room as your own.'

'I don't want to create any inconvenience.'

I looked to him. 'Nightmares have already driven him into my room. There is no bed for you, but I'm sure I can make some comfort on the floor.'

'It's a shame that the furniture here was taken,' said Hashi with a glance about the room.

'A fresh start,' I responded, my smile broadening.

'A fresh start,' he echoed with a nod.

* * *

We passed north through the countryside, still holding each other's hands as we made our way to the Olsens'. I wondered at Nicky's reaction. He had no idea that there was even the prospect of a man in my life and I was worried that he would not take too kindly to the invasion of our relationship. It was the core of his existence and now Hashi could be seen to threaten that bond.

'You worry,' stated Hashi.

I looked to him and found him studying my expression. 'About my son's reaction,' I replied openly.

'Worrying will not change what his reaction is,' he said.

'I know.' I turned my attention forward once more.

'His name is Nicholas, you say?'

'Yes, though he prefers Nicky.'

We continued in silence for a while. I tried to rein in my fretting, knowing that Hashi was right, that no amount of worrying would make any difference to the situation that arose. Instead, I focussed on the surroundings, the birdsong becoming sharper and the spring colours more vivid.

We walked amidst wild flowers, pushed through thickets and took to the shadows beneath woodland trees. I found a sense of contentment coming over me, one given additional depth by the touch of his hand.

'What should we name our first child?' asked Hashi out of the blue.

I looked to him in surprise and found him smiling at me, amusement in his eyes. 'As long as it is a name drawn from our own people, I do not care. Though if it is twins, I think we should call them Tohbi and Losa'

'Twins!' he exclaimed, both of us laughing.

'White and Black,' he added with a nod. 'They are good choices.'

I brought him to a halt through the link of our hands. 'I am glad you said those words to me yesterday,' I said, my expression becoming more serious. 'They cut away my illusions and brought me back to the present.'

'They rang true for me as well,' he admitted. 'It seems we were both holding onto something that had long let go of us.' His smile was tinged with sadness.

I reached up and stroked his cheek with the back of my free hand. 'You are man of depth and beauty.'

Hashi lifted my hand to his lips and kissed it. 'It seems we share many things.' His smile brightened and his eyes were filled with a light from which I wished no escape, their illumination felt within the halls of my heart.

We set off once again and I tried to spy landmarks which would help guide us to the farmstead. Thinking I could see the western hill of the vale, I knew there was not far to go.

My estimation was proved correct when we exited a strand of pine and saw the Olsens' house north of our position. I glanced at Hashi, concern rising to the fore of my mind once again as we began towards it and I looked for any sign of the Swedes or my son.

* * *

Chula's grip loosened as we drew closer to the low building. Finally releasing my hand, I knew she was worried about her boy's reaction to my presence. I tried not to think about it, but her apparent nervousness was infectious to a degree.

Apprehensively looking to the farmstead, I saw a woman in a pale yellow housedress appear at the door. A boy half her size came into view beside her, his native features clearly showing his African heritage. His hair was not straight, like that of our people, but tightly sprung, his nose wide and skin darker.

'He is his father's son,' I commented as he stepped out onto the porch, looking at us curiously.

The woman encouraged him forward with a gentle push, her lips moving, but her words failing to carry to us as we continued across the grassland. Nicky made his way towards us, his steps lacking confidence and his eyes regarding me uneasily.

'Who's that?' he asked when within ten yards, his pace slowing and coming to a stop.

'This is Hashi,' introduced Chula. 'He is a good friend.'

The boy cocked his head to the side. 'You haven't mentioned him before.'

'That is because we only recently met,' she replied as we neared him.

'It's good to meet you, Nicky,' I greeted, holding out my hand.

He looked to Chula questioningly and she gave a shallow nod. Taking my hand, we shook. 'Doesn't Hashi mean 'moon'?' he asked.

I nodded. 'It seems your mother is teaching you well or you're a good learner.'

'Both,' he replied with growing confidence. 'Do you like oat cakes?'

His question was unexpected and I glanced at Chula, who I discovered grinning at me. 'Very much,' I replied.

'Not as much as this little man,' she said, rubbing his hair affectionately.

'Marie flavours them with honey,' he said conversationally, his initial uncertainty apparently already gone.

'Does she indeed?' I responded, glancing at the woman who remained in the doorway. 'My mouth is already watering at the thought of tasting one.'

Nicky smiled. 'You can have two, if you like.'

Chula chuckled. 'They are not really yours to offer.'

'Marie made them especially for me,' he said, turning to his mother as a golden hound came bounding around the corner of the house, heading straight towards us.

I took a step backward as the dog stopped beside the boy, bearing its teeth and growling at me, hackles raised along its spine.

'He's a friend, Honung,' said Nicky, Chula looking at me with the unmistakable glisten of tears in her eyes, made happy by her son's quick acceptance of my presence.

'Let her sniff your hand,' said the boy as he placated the hound by stroking her.

I moved forward and slowly put out my hand. She sniffed, hackles lowering and expression softening. Licking my fingers, she proceeded to sniff at my boots and britches.

'You see, she's fine,' said Nicky brightly, the dog's approval adding to his own.

'Let us go see Marie and Anders,' stated Chula, taking Nicky's hand.

They set off towards the house and she looked over her shoulder, beckoning for me to join them. I quickly caught up and, to my surprise, she took hold of my hand once again.

'Do you live at the settlement?' asked Nicky, looking around his mother and noting our bond with a brief expression of interest, glancing up at her face.

'I did,' I replied.

'Where do you live now?'

'Hashi will be coming to live with us, as long as you do not mind,' stated Chula, her grip about my hand tightening.

'He can stay in my room,' suggested Nicky happily.

'That is what I thought,' she replied with relief in her tone.

'Will you stay with us for long?'

'He may be with us for quite some time,' she said as we reached the porch. 'Hashi, this is Marie Olsen. She and her husband are more than just friends, they are family.'

'Pleased to meet you,' I said, releasing Chula's hand and holding mine out towards the woman.

Her eyes displayed the same emotion I had recently seen in Chula's. Glancing at my hand, she then stepped forward and took me into a brief embrace. 'It is so very good to meet you,' she responded, her words accented and looking away as she tried to subtly wipe away a stray tear.

'Come in,' she said, clearing her throat and composing herself as she went into the house.

'Is Auntie Marie all right?' asked Nicky, craning his neck to look up at his mother.

'She is fine,' responded Chula, letting go of his hand and indicating for him to enter first.

Waiting until he'd passed inside, she turned to me and looked into my eyes. 'Everything is going to be fine,' she stated, her smile softening. 'We are going to be fine.'

'Here.'

We turned to find Nicky standing in the doorway holding out an oak cake. Glancing at each other in amusement, I then took it from the boy and raised it to my nose, sniffing deeply.

'Smells delicious.'

'It tastes even better,' he said, watching in eager anticipation as I took my first bite.

* * *

We sat around the table to eat lunch. Hashi was using an upturned bucket for a seat, there being only four chairs. Nicky found his much diminished height amusing and Hashi played up to it, staying stooped and reaching up for his bread and cheese with exaggerated awkwardness that made the boy chuckle. I noticed a wink pass between them and my heart was warmed by the sight.

'What work is it you do?' asked Anders.

'I've been helping people with various jobs,' replied Hashi, straightening as he sat between me and the Swede.

'It may be I will have some work you can be helping me with from time to time, if you have need.'

'Thank you,' replied Hashi. 'That would be a kindness.'

'You can watch me ride after we've eaten,' stated Nicky.

'That sounds like a fine idea,' he smiled at the boy. 'I bet you're a natural.'

'That's what Uncle Anders says.' Nicky beamed.

There was a brief silence as we ate our simple meal and washed it down with water drawn from the Olsens' well.

'That was good,' said Hashi. 'Was that wild garlic and basil in the bread?'

Marie nodded as she swallowed a mouthful of water and set her cup down. 'I thought the flavours would compliment the bread well.'

'And you were right.'

'Not as good as the oat cakes,' commented Nicky.

'We all know they are your favourite,' I said, grinning at him. 'You would have Marie baking them all day long if you could.'

'And all night,' he added.

'Should we fetch Rödbeta out?' asked Anders.

Nicky gave a nod and turned sideways before jumping from his chair. He hurried to the door and put on his boots, Honung joining him. 'Ready.'

All the adults laughed.

'As quick as lightening,' stated Anders as he rose from his seat and went to join the boy.

They soon exited, closing the door on the strengthening wind.

'Where do you live?' asked Marie as the sound of Nicky's laughter drifted into the house mingled with the dog's playful bark.

'I've a farm,' replied Hashi, glancing at me.

'He is going to be moving in with us,' I revealed. 'He can use Nicky's room.'

Marie looked at me, her eyes expressing her happiness.

'Do you suppose Anders would be willing to help me construct a bed?' asked Hashi.

'I'm sure he would. Have you the wood?'

He shook his head.

'No matter. He could take you to the hardware store on the cart,' she offered.

'I've no money,' he replied, his expression becoming thoughtful. 'Maybe he'd accompany me to my farm. We could take down a couple of fence posts and some sidings in order to make one.'

Marie looked at him in puzzlement. 'You don't intend to go back at some point?'

Hashi glanced at me and reached for my hand. 'Our union will make me an outcast,' he said in explanation, his act of taking hold reassuring me that his newfound status was of no consequence.

Marie nodded in understanding. 'I will speak with him about it and am sure he'll be happy to help.'

She stood and collected up the plates, Hashi keeping hold of my hand. Stepping to the stove, she took up the pail of water beside and brought it over with a small cloth taken from the dresser in readiness to clean the crockery.

'Ishki!'

We all looked to the window to discover Nicky sitting atop Rödbeta outside. I got up, the bond between Hashi and I coming apart as I went to the door. Marie dropped the cloth on the tabletop and we all passed out onto the porch; a small audience lining up in readiness for the performance.

I glanced back and considered collecting my cloak, thankful that the house protected us from the full force of the wind.

'You look like you belong up there,' commented Hashi.

'Watch me,' he called down, taking the horse's mane and turning her south.

'Be careful,' I said as he set off, nervous at the sight of him riding bare back.

Rödbeta trotted and Nicky turned to us, lifting both hands in the air and waving.

'Keep hold,' I shouted.

Leaning forward and taking the mane in both hands, Nicky used his heels to get the horse to build up speed. Lowering himself against Rödbeta's neck, she began to gallop across the grassland.

I jumped at the feel of Hashi's fingers taking my hand and glanced at him, finding him smiling at me as he tried to alleviate my tension.

A pheasant suddenly took flight from the grass ahead of the horse, flapping and calling in alarm. Rödbeta pulled up dramatically, given a fright by the bird.

Nicky was thrown from the horse's back. Passing over its head with a scream, he sailed through the air and thumped down into the grass. His body all but hidden, there was no sign of movement.

'NICKY!' I yelled, immediately leaping from the porch, my hand tearing from Hashi's as I began to sprint to my son's still form.

I glanced to my left when I saw movement at the edge of my vision. Anders was also making for Nicky, Honung at his side and face stricken with horror as Rödbeta tossed her head with nervous agitation at our approach.

'Nicky?' I called, my mouth thick with phlegm as I neared and heard a groan issue from his prone form.

I went to his side, crouching and reaching for him in order to roll him onto his back.

'No,' stated Anders, lowering himself onto his haunches on the other side of my son. 'It is best not to move him until we know his injuries.'

'Nicky, can you hear me?' I asked, my voice filled with panicked concern as the Swede took Honung by the scruff of the neck to stop her going to him.

He let out another groan and slowly rolled himself over as Hashi and Marie joined us, standing beyond the boy's feet. 'Darn pheasant,' he croaked as he slowly sat up, a grass stain along the right side of his face and a swelling beginning to form beneath.

I stared at him, feeling sickened and my heart thumping in the wake of the scare. Gathering him into my arms, I held him tightly.

'Ouch!'

I released him, hands to his shoulders as I looked to his face. 'What is wrong?'

'My ribs hurt,' he stated.

I lifted his shirt, seeing bruising beginning to darken his skin on the side of his ribcage that corresponded with the grass stain. I tested to see if any ribs might be broken with my fingertips, but detected no such injury.

'Why did you not reply when I called out your name?' I asked as I let his shirt fall back into place.

'The fall knocked the air from my lungs,' he replied, clearly feeling a little embarrassed as we all remained gathered about him and he looked to his feet.

* * *

I looked down upon Chula and Nicky as Anders straightened and went to the horse. The Swede approached it with care, the creature still uneasy and sniffing the hand that he offered as he softly spoke her name. He patted and stroked her neck, Rödbeta tossing her head and snorting as I turned back to the boy sitting amidst the grass.

'The fall knocked the air from my lungs,' he repeated, shaking his head as if a fly had gone into his ear.

'You have already told us,' said Chula as Nicky went to rise.

She put her arm about him and helped the boy to his feet.

'Can we have oat cakes?' he asked, looking to Marie while inserting a finger into one of his ears. 'What's that noise?'

'What noise?'

'That ringing noise?'

Chula looked at him with concern. 'We should get you back to the house.'

He took a step forward, his mother offering her help. 'I can manage,' he snapped with surprising force, Marie and I sharing a glance.

Nicky passed between us and headed towards the building. His feet dragged as he shook his head again and stumbled.

His legs giving way beneath him, he suddenly toppled forward. Thumping to the ground once again, he lay still upon his front, face buried in the grass.

I rushed to him, turning him over as Chula and Marie joined me.

'What is wrong with him?' asked Chula fearfully, the boy's eyes closed and face pale.

'I don't know,' I admitted.

'Nicky?' she asked, gathering him onto her lap, his head resting on her arm. 'Nicky?'

There was no sign of life other than the shallow rise and fall of his chest.

She looked up at me with desperation in her dark eyes. 'Help him,' she pleaded.

'We must carry him inside,' said Anders, coming over to stand by his wife. He looked to me and I nodded.

'You must let us take him,' I said to Chula as she continued to grasp her son.

She seemed not to hear me, her head bowed as she stared at his face, the swelling upon his cheek becoming more prominent.

'Chula,' I said softly, placing my hand on her arm as she began to caress Nicky's face with the backs of her fingers.

She looked to me, terror in her eyes.

'Let me and Anders get him inside,' I reiterated. 'It's cold out here and we must get him warm and comfortable.'

Chula turned her attention back to her son, stroking his cheek one last time before reluctantly releasing him to us.

I took him beneath the arms as Anders moved to his feet and grasped the boy at the ankles. We lifted him from the grass and headed towards the house with Honung padding beside, Chula kneeling on the grass staring after us as Marie went to her side.

I looked back over my shoulder to see the Swedish woman place her arm about Chula's shoulders, getting her to her feet.

'I do not know what I would do without him,' stated Chula as they began to follow.

'You will not be without him,' reassured Marie.

We neared the porch and slowed. Chula and Marie drew up alongside, the latter going to the door and opening it.

Entering, Chula grasped Nicky's hand as we took him along the hall and entered the bedroom on the left. Marie bustled in behind us, quickly pulling back the covers and placing one pillow atop the other.

Turning so that I could rest the boy's head on the pillows, Anders and I then set him down. I stepped back, Nicky seeming as though he were in a deep sleep as Marie drew the covers over him and Chula stood beside the bed with his hand still clasped in hers.

'I'll fetch a seat,' said Anders, exiting the room and soon returning with one of the chairs from about the table.

He set it beside Chula near the head of the bed.

'Sit,' said Marie, gently resting her hand on Chula's shoulder.

She sat down as if in a daze, taking Nicky's hand to her lap and holding it in both of hers. Rubbing his skin with her thumb in nervous agitation, tears began to fall.

Her distress took me to her side, my heart yearning to bring her what comfort I could. Crouching beside the chair as Marie moved to stand at the foot of the bed, I put my hand on her forearm. 'All will be well.'

She turned, eyes desolate and face awash. 'How?' she asked, her tone filled with a plea for me to assuage her fear.

'Time,' I stated. 'He needs time to recover.'

'Go to the town and seek out the doctor,' said Marie, looking to her husband.

'We could put him on the cart,' responded Anders.

Marie shook her head. 'We don't know what causes his condition and being jolted on the bed of the cart may make things worse. Ride quickly and fetch him.'

He nodded and passed out of the room. 'I will be back as soon as I can,' he called down the corridor, his steps quick as he made his way to the front door.

'Would you like some water?' asked Marie

Chula gave a nod and the Swede went to the door, pausing before stepping out of the room.

'I should stay with you,' I stated.

She looked to me, eyes filled with sadness. 'Would you mind if I am left alone with him?' Her body trembled as she fought against the urge to break down.

I shook my head, tightening the grip on her arm momentarily and then getting to my feet. Marie re-entered carrying a cup. I stepped aside and she handed it to Chula.

'Thank you,' she said, taking it to her lips and drinking deep, passing the empty vessel back to her.

'More?'

Chula shook her head.

Marie made to leave the room again. I hesitated and she touched my arm to get my attention.

'Let us leave her in peace,' she said softly, her eyes filled with compassion.

I reluctantly followed her out of the room, Marie stepping to the side and pulling the door to once I'd vacated.

'Come,' she said, linking her arm in mine and taking me along the hall to the main room as the sounds of Chula's sobs emanated from the bedroom at our backs.

* * *

I sat by the bed and wept for a long time. Holding onto Nicky's hand and wailing softly, I rocked back and forth. The image of Ishki in her rocking chair came to mind and I finally understood how grief had caused her to stow herself away, its outward expression in the motion of the chair.

Lifting his fingers to my lips, I kissed them. 'Please come back to me,' I stated through my misery, sniffing and blinking in an attempt to clear my vision.

'Maybe I am being punished,' I said, looking to my son's face.

Inki and Akocha blamed me for Ishki's passing and it could be that blame was well placed. I had also recently released my hold on Nicholas, something that could be deemed a betrayal, though my love for him would remain while I had breath. Was the Great Spirit judging me? Was this retribution of the kind the Christ worshippers talked about?

I shook my head, trying to clear such unhelpful thoughts from my mind. 'I was motivated by love,' I whispered. 'Would you punish me for such?'

'Ishki?' said Nicky groggily, his lids lifting halfway.

'Nicky!' I looked at him in surprise.

He turned his head, at first looking at my hands about his and then to my face. 'What happened?'

'You passed out,' I stated. 'Now you must rest.'

'I remember being thrown from Rödbeta, but nothing after.'

'There is little after to be remembered,' I responded, stroking the back of his hand.

He licked his lips. 'My mouth is dry.'

'I will call Marie and she can get you some water.'

'Marie?' His expression became puzzled.

'The Swedish woman,' I replied, worried that he may have lost his memory.

'I know who Auntie Marie is,' he said, 'I just thought we were home.'

'Not yet,' I said, relieved that his mind did not seem affected by the fall. 'We will be going back once the doctor has seen you.'

'With Hashi?'

I nodded.

'I like him,' he stated. 'I'm glad you found him, Ishki.' The faintest of smiles curled his lips as he looked at me.

'We found each other,' I replied, thinking his words apt, both me and Hashi having been lost to the past until so recently. 'I will call for some water.'

I turned for the door just as it opened.

'I thought I heard voices and am glad to find I was correct,' said Marie as she peered in and smiled at the sight of Nicky's wakefulness.

'Would you mind fetching him some water?'

'Not at all,' she replied, turning and hurrying along the hall.

A few mumbled words were exchanged in the main room and she soon returned with Hashi close behind. Marie made her way over and handed me the cup, a little of the liquid escaping over the side.

'I'm glad to see you've decided to join us. If you weren't back soon I was going to wave oat cakes under your nose to wake you,' joked Hashi as I held the cup out to my son.

Nicky grinned as he struggled to sit up. Hashi stepped to the opposite side of the bed and helped him.

'Are you all right?' he asked the boy, a hand supportively to his back.

Nicky nodded and took the cup from me, lifting it to his lips and drinking deeply. Taking a gasping breath, he lowered it to his lap and cradled it.

'Do you have any pain?' asked Marie.

'My chest hurts and my cheek throbs,' he replied, his words attesting to the two injuries we had already detected.

'Nothing else?' I asked.

'It's just a little hard to think straight.'

'That will get better in time,' reassured Hashi as steps sounded in the hall.

Anders appeared in the doorway, leading the white doctor from the settlement into the room.

'This is Doctor Staples,' introduced the Swede.

'I take it this is the boy you were telling me about,' said the rangy doctor, his beady eyes already examining his prospective patient.

'That's him,' confirmed Anders.

'It's very crowded in here,' stated Staples as he neatened his thinning brown hair after the disturbance of the wind.

'Come on,' said Marie, taking Anders by the sleeve of his dark coat and leading him out of the room.

'Are you the mother?' asked Staples.

'Yes. My name's Chula.'

'May I?' he asked, stepping to my side of the bed.

I moved out of the way and went round to join Hashi as the doctor placed his leather bag on the floor and took the seat I had been sitting on. He placed his hand to Nicky's brow to test his temperature.

'I hear you had quite a fall,' he stated without friendliness.

Nicky nodded.

'Is that the only bruising?' He looked to the boy's inflamed cheek.

'He has bruised ribs,' I stated.

'Lift your shirt,' said Staples without glancing at me.

Nicky did as instructed and the doctor stared at the injury momentarily before raising a hand to it. He prodded and felt with his fingers. 'Painful?'

'A little,' said Nicky, flinching from time to time.

'You'll be glad to hear nothing is broken,' stated the doctor. 'I was told he passed out,' he said, finally looking at me.

'Yes. He got up after being thrown from the horse and then passed out.'

'When he came off the horse, did he land on his head?'

'It may be so.'

The doctor turned his attention back to Nicky. 'How's your head feeling?'

'Like it's thick with fog,' he replied, 'and I feel tired.'

'Any ringing in your ears, weakness or sensitivity to light?'

'There was ringing in his ears after he fell,' stated Hashi.

The doctor sighed and nodded. 'As I thought.'

'What did you think?' I asked.

'He has likely suffered a concussion,' said Staples. 'He needs bed rest and someone should stay with him for the next couple of days. He should avoid any strenuous activity for the time being and there should be no more riding until he is fully recovered.'

'How long should it take?'

'A few days,' said the doctor with a noncommittal shrug. 'Keep an eye out for changes in personality or difficulty in understanding. If you notice any such things, make sure to send someone for me.'

He picked up his bag and rose from the chair.

'Is that it?' asked Hashi.

'There is nothing else I can to. Rest is the best treatment in such cases.' He walked alongside the bed and paused at the foot. 'Make sure he doesn't overly exert himself,' he reiterated before going to the door and passing along the hall.

I quickly moved from Hashi's side and went to the doorway. 'Doctor?' I called after him as he passed across the main room.

He stopped and looked back at me questioningly.

'Can we move him?'

'As long as he's not put under any stress,' he replied before continuing to the door. 'Good day to you all,' he said over his shoulder as he stepped out onto the porch and closed the portal after him.

Marie and Anders came into view.

'What did he say?' she asked.

'Not much,' I responded with a frown.

'We are not part of the reservation,' stated Anders. 'I had to persuade him to come.'

'And he couldn't wait to get back.'

'What treatment did he suggest?'

'Bed rest until he is feeling himself again. Would it be all right if you take us home on the cart?'

Anders gave a nod. 'Do you wish to go soon?'

'It would probably be for the best. I want to get him back and settled.'

'I'll go and put the harness on Rödbeta,' he said, making for the door. 'I'll bring the cart round to the front.'

'Thank you,' I responded as he stepped out.

* * *

'If you come by in the morning, we'll see to fetching timber from your farm,' said Anders as we approached Chula's house.

'Thank you,' I replied as I sat next to him on the driver's bench, Chula seated in the cart with Nicky cuddled into her side.

He pulled on the reins and Rödbeta circled the cart so it faced south before coming to a halt beside the gate. The thud of hooves drew my gaze down the vale and I saw three horsemen approaching.

Shading my eyes, I found Duncan riding at the centre, a spare mount trailing behind him on a lead rope. To the right rode Forrester and on the other side of my brother was my cousin, Stephen, all three men with grim expressions.

'Help Chula get the boy into the house,' I instructed Anders before jumping down.

Moving to stand a few yards before the cart, I waited. My pulse became elevated and Rödbeta whinnied as the three riders drew closer.

'Hashi?'

I looked over my shoulder to see Chula standing by the back of the cart, a fretful look upon her face.

'Get Nicky inside. I'll deal with this,' I said, trying not to betray my nervousness. 'The doctor said he must avoid stress or strain.'

'I should stand beside you,' she said.

'Your son's health is more important. Get him into the house and I'll join you shortly.'

She hesitated and then went to help Nicky down from the cart, Anders waiting in readiness.

Facing forward, I found my brother only twenty yards away. Duncan watched Chula and Anders take the boy through the gate and along the path as he slowed his mount and came to a halt.

'What brings you here?' I asked, looking up at him.

'We have come to take you back, Brother.'

'I've made my choice,' I replied as I heard the front door shut, relieved that Chula was safely inside.

'I went to see Bartholomew. He knows the medicine of our people and says you are under a spell.'

'He's nothing but a washed out drunk,' I replied. 'There's only one spell I am under, and that is love.'

Duncan shook his head sorrowfully. 'You may think it's so, but he consulted the spirits. The outcast has you bewitched and we're taking you back so that he may undo her enchantment.'

'I'm not going anywhere,' I insisted, holding his gaze.

He frowned at me. 'I hoped it would not come to this.' He nodded first to Forrester and then to Stephen.

They dismounted and began to approach me with purpose, a length of rope held in Forrester's weathered hands. I took a step back, muscles coiled as I prepared to fight.

'Forrester. Stephen,' I said, looking at them in turn. 'This is not your quarrel.'

'You are family, Cousin,' replied Stephen, who was in his early twenties and was wearing a stovepipe hat on his long greasy hair. 'We will not let you become an outcast too.'

They continued to close on me. I thought about running, but could not bring myself to abandon Chula. The thought of her or the boy coming to harm churned my stomach. There was only one real option open to me; I would have to leave with my brother to ensure her safety.

'I will come,' I stated, holding my hands up in submission, 'but there is a condition.'

'You're not in a position to negotiate,' responded Duncan, the cattle farmer and my cousin coming to a halt to either side of me.

'If my feelings remain the same after we've visited with Bartholomew, you will let me return,' I stated, ignoring his dismissal. 'I can see no reason for you to refuse if you believe I'm under a spell that he can break.'

Duncan considered a moment. 'You will come peaceably?'

'I will.'

'Then I'll let you leave peaceably if Bartholomew's medicine has no effect,' he conceded.

Despite my limited faith in his agreement and the possibility that I may still have to make good an escape, I made my way towards the spare horse. Passing Duncan, I didn't look up at him as Forrester and Stephen went to their mounts and climbed up into the saddles.

I took hold of the creature's mane and pulled myself up, my brother watching over his shoulder. When I was settled, he nudged his horse in the flanks and we turned. Setting off through the vale, I looked back at the house, seeing Chula's face at the window partly obscured by clouds gathering to the north.

* * *

I watched them leave. Seeing Hashi look back, I raised my hand to the glass. He raised his hand in kind and then turned away, the four riders diminishing into the south and my heart aching at the sight.

'Anowa chipisala' cho,' I whispered.

I had heard the exchange outside and wondered at the result of visiting with the old medicine man. I had cast no intentional spell, knew only a little of the medicine that had once guided our people, but wondered at the means of persuasion that would be used to try and turn Hashi's heart from me.

'He will be back,' stated Anders as he joined me at the window and looked out at the shrinking shapes of the riders in the sunlight.

'I'd better return home,' he added, looking to the cloud coming from the north. 'Unless you have need of me here.' He looked at me and saw my anguish.

'He loves you, that is plain to see.' He placed a comforting hand upon my shoulder.

'Is it enough?'

Anders held my gaze. 'There is nothing they can do to expel it from his heart, for it resides deep.'

'I hope you are right.'

'I know I am,' he stated with confidence. 'Nicky is settled upon his bed and Marie told me to give you this.'

210

He produced a cloth-wrapped package from inside his coat.

I took it from him and pulled back the folds to reveal the last of the oat cakes.

'She thought it would help his recovery and his mood,' he said with a smile.

'I am sure it will. Please pass on my thanks.'

He removed his hand. 'Do you want me to stay?' he reiterated.

I shook my head. 'You should get back to Marie,' I replied, wanting company, but not wishing to ask more of him after all he had done.

He regarded me a moment, as if knowing I was merely being considerate. 'I could make the fire before I go,' he suggested.

'That would be appreciated.'

He gave a nod and moved to the hearth. Taking up the poker, he began to corral the ash through the bottom grate in order to clear the way for a new fire.

I looked back to the view from the window. No longer able to see the riders, I reluctantly moved away and went across the room. Passing down the hall, I went into the room that Nicky and I shared, finding him sitting in his bed with his back to the wall and pillow between.

'How are you feeling?' I asked, crouching beside him.

'Tired,' he responded, eyes hooded.

'Then you should get some rest,' I stated.

'Are they oat cakes?' he asked, seeing the package in my hands.

I lifted them into plain sight. 'Marie sent the last of them with Anders.'

'Can I have one?'

I smiled. 'Of course.' I held them out to him and Nicky took the nearest, smelling it before taking a bite.

'Would you like some water?'

He nodded as he ate.

'We will save the rest until later or you will finish them in a flash.'

'Who were those men?' he asked after swallowing, taking another bite as soon as the question had passed his lips.

My smile vanished and I glanced at the rearward window. 'One was Hashi's brother.'

'What did they want?'

'They have taken him back to the settlement for a while,' I stated.

Nicky looked at me with his head cocked to the side and the half eaten cake held before his mouth. 'Why?'

'Family matters.'

'He is coming back, isn't he?'

'Yes,' I said, looking to his eyes and trying to inject my answer with a certainty that I did not feel in truth.

'We should save him an oat cake,' he said thoughtfully and with a glance to those remaining on my hand, the edges of the cloth draped over the side.

'That is a good idea,' I said with forced cheer. 'I will put these someplace safe and fetch you some water.'

I stood and went to the door.

'Thank you, Ishki.'

Turning, I found Nicky smiling at me while stifling a yawn.

A swell of emotion arose as a result of all that had happened that afternoon and I bit back tears. 'I love you.'

'I love you too,' he responded.

Lingering a moment as he settled himself on the bed, I then made my way out into the hall. Hashi came to mind and I yearned for the security of his embrace.

The sharp striking of a match gave me a start as I entered the main room. I found Anders crouched before the fire, taking the new flame to the kindling he had put in place.

'How is he?' he enquired, looking over at me as the flames became established.

'Tired, but well,' I responded, going to the dresser and taking down a cup to fill at the bucket. 'Could you fetch some more water before you leave? The doctor said not to leave Nicky and I would prefer to remain at the house.'

He straightened as the sunlight began to diminish, the clouds drawing across the sky. 'Should I shut the chicken coop while I am outside?'

'Thank you,' I said with a nod.

Bending, I filled the cup from what remained in the bucket. Placing it on the table, I took up a large earthenware bowl and poured the last of the water into it, holding the empty bucket out to Anders as he crossed the room.

Taking it, he went to the door and exited the house. My gaze went to the window. I looked south, knowing that the riders were long gone, but some part of me hoping to see Hashi on his return. There was no one in sight as the late afternoon continued to darken and I sighed regretfully.

'May he soon come back to us,' I said, taking the cup from the table and making my way from the room.

* * *

We passed through the settlement, my brother leading the way with Forrester and Stephen riding behind so that there was little chance of my escape if I should choose to take flight. Heads turned and eyes watched questioningly, the town subdued in the cold greyness that had drawn down from the north.

Riding by the bench before the Exchange, I looked down upon a couple of men seated together sharing a jug of the moonshine Wilson had been selling. They stared back at me with bloodshot eyes, their spirit taken by the drink. One tried to take the jug from the other after lowering his gaze, his companion quickly looking down and holding on tightly, hugging the container to his chest as they began to tussle.

'That was you not so long ago,' commented Duncan.

I found him looking over his shoulder at me as the drunks continued to squabble. 'Not anymore,' I replied. 'I know my own mind,' I added, suspecting that was his implication.

'You seek to replace one addiction with another,' he stated.

I said nothing in response, seeing the shack at the outskirts of the settlement ahead, separated from the last of the other buildings by a patch of scrubland. Smoke could be seen issuing from the chimney and escaping the confines through numerous cracks, shrouding the ramshackle building and giving it the appearance of existing between this world and the next.

We rode onto the edge of the scrub and the horses were brought to a halt. My escorts quickly dismounted, keeping a wary eye on me as I slowly climbed down.

Leading the way once again, Duncan walked around to the front of the building. Entering, Forrester and Stephen remained by the door, the latter closing it as my brother moved to stand by the fire that was burning in the central pit.

The air was filled with smoke which swirled in numerous draughts. Standing on the far side of the pit was Bartholomew. He wore a black mask and a tatty cloak of leaves, holding a fan of feathers as the fumes moved about him. It was as if I were looking at a vision from the past as he stood ready to practice the medicine of our people.

'Payment,' he stated to my brother, words muffled by the mask.

Duncan reached into his coat, taking a small bottle of whisky from the inside pocket and passing it to Bartholomew's waiting hand. It was tucked within the folds of his ragged clothes and I noticed his hand shaking.

'Sit before the flames,' said the old man, turning to me as he picked up a bundle of dried herbs that were resting on the furs where he usually sat and threw them onto the flames.

I did as instructed, sure that his show would have no effect and doubtful that it was anything more than a charade performed for the benefit of the alcohol he had been promised as payment. Sitting cross-legged, I watched as he began to wave the feathers and chant, raising his hands high into the haze. A bracelet of bones rattled upon his wrist as he began to prance about the fire, Duncan moving back as Bartholomew passed behind me.

He danced around a few times and came to a stop opposite me, raising his hands up once again and the sound of the bones mingling with those of the fire. I coughed and my eyes watered. Blinking them clear, I saw him nod towards my cousin and the cattle farmer.

Before I had a chance to react, they were upon me. They each took hold of an arm, securing them behind my back as my brother came forward. He opened my coat and undid the buttons of my shirt, baring my chest.

Bartholomew bent to the fire, taking up a length of charred timber from the edge of the flames. He prowled around the side of the pit and came to me, all the while chanting.

Leaning over me, he placed the glowing tip to my chest. I tensed and gritted my teeth against the pain, Forrester and Stephen increasing the strength of their hold in response.

Passing it across my skin, the burnt timber left black marks, my muscles jumping beneath its passage. Perspiration dripped down my face as the old man created a number of symbols upon my chest, the mask grinning down at me.

Pausing, he suddenly pushed the tip hard against my flesh in the location of my heart. My head snapped back and I let out a long cry of pain, my throat taut and tendons bulging.

Bartholomew quickly tossed the burnt piece of wood into the fire and held his hands above my mouth, making ushering movements as if encouraging my breath upward. 'The poison she put in his heart has vacated,' he announced.

He stepped away, his right foot catching the stones at the edge of the pit and causing him to stumble. 'Her spell has been undone,' he stated after recovering his balance, hand already reaching inside his clothes for the whisky.

'How do you feel?' asked Duncan as he knelt at my side, my assailants' grip loosening on my arms.

I stared at him, my chest searing with pain. 'You brought me here for this?' I shook my head. 'I don't know who is more the fool, him or you?' I added, looking to Bartholomew as he unscrewed the lid and raised the bottle to his lips after pushing the mask to the top of his head, his face dripping with sweat.

Duncan glanced at the old man.

'If it hasn't worked,' began Bartholomew, lowering the bottle and wiping his lips with the back of his hand, 'then he is too deep under her spell and too far removed from the Nation.'

'What of the outcast?' enquired my brother, regarding me closely. 'What do you feel towards her?'

I blinked away sweat, my eyes stinging and the skin blistering where the old man had pressed the tip to my chest. 'I love her, Brother,' I stated, holding his gaze.

'Her spell is too deep,' stated Bartholomew before raising the bottle to his lips again, trying to finish it in case it was demanded back in sight of his failure.

'You can't,' said Duncan.

'I do,' I affirmed.

I pulled my arms from Stephen and Forrester's grip. Looking down at my chest, I drew my shirt closed over the marks and blistering, doing up the buttons with tremulous hands. Turning my attention back to Duncan, I saw the expression of dismay upon his face.

I reached out and took a firm hold of his wrist. 'I love you too, Brother, but I am going to return to her. It's your choice as to whether you see me as an outcast or not.'

'No good will come of it.'

'So you choose outcast,' I stated sadly, getting to my feet and backing away. 'If you should ever change your mind, I'll be waiting to embrace you,' I added, looking down at him.

I stepped towards the door. Stephen and Forrester moved to bar my way, poised to take me into their custody.

I looked back at Duncan as he remained kneeling by the pit, a desolate expression upon his face. 'Brother?'

He slowly turned to me.

'Will you force me to remain? Will you take away my liberty and keep me a prisoner the rest of my days?'

He took a deep breath and nodded at his companions, who stepped aside.

'You are a fool,' stated Forrester. 'You would turn your back on your people?'

'It's they who are turning their back on me,' I countered. 'All I am doing is following the call of my heart.'

He shook his head. 'And by doing so you break your brother's.'

'That is his choice.' I stepped between them and opened the door on the gloom of early evening, the clouds heavy overhead.

With a parting glance as the smoke billowed out about me, I closed the portal and walked away, thankful to be free of the choking confines and thoughts already turning to Chula.

* * *

I sat beside the pillow at the head of the bed, leaning against the wall as I stroked Nicky's cheek, more for my comfort than his, the boy fast asleep. The late afternoon was fast passing into evening as the wind moaned through a gap about the window. I thought about Hashi, worried that he would not return and hoping that he was not under duress as his brother tried to persuade him to abandon me.

'I'm hungry.'

I looked down to find Nicky awake, though the stain of weariness marked his eyes. 'What would you like? I could make fried eggs on bread,' I suggested.

'Yes, thank you,' he said, yawning.

I wiped away a tear from his cheek and got to my feet. 'Do you need help to rise or should I get the fire going in the stove?'

'I'll be fine,' he replied. 'Is Hashi home?'

I shook my head. 'Soon,' I replied, praying I was right.

Waiting until he had stood to be sure he was steady upon his feet, I exited and made my way along the hallway. Seeing the fire in the hearth was low, I quickly went over and placed some of the last logs onto the meagre flames. Looking at the woodpile, I realised that lighting the stove would leave little by which to keep us warm during the night, but did not want to disappoint Nicky after promising fried eggs.

'I will fry them in the hearth,' I stated to myself as the new logs hissed.

Trying to push thoughts of Hashi from my mind, knowing that fretting would not bring him to the door, I went to the dresser and took down the skillet. Hunting out a handful of eggs, I took them over to the fireplace and rested them on the floor.

Returning to the table, I set two plates upon it. Pausing, I reached for a third and was just transferring it to the tabletop when there was a knock at the door.

I hastened over and opened it excitedly.

Essy stood before me, a cloth-covered dish upon her right hand.

'Hello, Nora,' she said with a tight smile.

I stared at her in surprise. 'You promised Akocha,' I stated.

'I promised him you would not visit with me again, but said nothing about visiting you,' she replied. 'Can I come in, the wind is biting?'

I stepped back and she entered.

'I've brought this for my nephew,' she said, holding the plate out to me, the edges of the cloth tucked beneath so as not to be taken by the wind.

I took it from her and lifted the pale cotton, seeing one of her sponge cakes beneath. 'He will be…'

'Auntie Essy!' exclaimed Nicky as he came out of the hall, hurrying over and embracing her.

'Do not get too excited, you know what the doctor said,' I warned.

'Doctor?' She looked to me.

'I fell from Rödbeta,' he stated, craning his neck to look up at her as he continued to hug his aunt.

'A horse?'

He nodded. 'The doctor says I have concussion.'

'I can see the bruise on your cheek. I hope it doesn't hurt too much.'

'Not too much,' he confirmed, finally stepping back from her.

'Can we have a slice of cake?' he asked as he came to inspect the result of my sister's baking, peeking beneath the cloth and inhaling deeply.

'After we have had the eggs,' I replied before turning my attention back to Essy. 'I did not think to find you out at this time. Where is Nathan?'

'Delphi has been taken ill and he's visiting her. If he returns before me, I will tell him I needed some air.'

'I hope it is not serious.'

'Knowing her, it is merely a chill that has been exaggerated into a matter of life and death,' answered Essy with a grin.

I looked at her affectionately. Placing the plate on the table, I stepped over and took her into my arms, holding her tight. 'I am so glad to see you.'

She held me close. 'And I you,' she replied.

We parted and I blinked tears from my eyes, not having expected to see my sister again. 'Will you stay for a while?'

'I can't this time, but will linger on future visits. I just wanted you to know that our contact has not come to an end.'

'Thank you.'

'Are you expecting a guest?' Her gaze settled on the three plates resting upon the table.

'Hashi and I…' I found myself unable to finish as I glanced out of the window, the fear that he would not come back stilling my tongue.

Essy's eyebrows rose in response, but she said nothing, not wishing to sour our reunion.

'Inki came,' I stated simply, clearing my throat and trying to distract myself.

'Here?' She looked at me in shock.

I nodded. 'He wanted to speak with me one last time.'

Essy turned her gaze to the floor. 'He is becoming increasingly morbid, but with it comes a greater contemplation of his life. He has said things to me I never thought to hear pass his lips.'

'Such as?'

She lifted her gaze. 'That he loves me and wishes he had been a better father when we were young. What did he say to you?'

'I think he just wanted to say goodbye in some way.'

'He isn't a well man.'

We fell into a brief and thoughtful silence.

'I should go,' she stated. 'Can I call on Monday morning?'

'It would be good to see you,' I replied.

'Could you bring another cake?' asked Nicky enthusiastically.

'Seeing as my favourite nephew needs to recover his health,' she answered with smile renewed.

'I'm your only nephew,' he stated.

'So you must be my favourite,' retorted Essy.

Nicky chuckled and she stepped to the door.

I moved to hug her again, feeling overwhelming gratitude in light of our continuing bond. We held each other and Nicky joined us, embracing us both and burying his head between.

'I will see you on Monday,' I stated as we parted.

'Until Monday,' she replied with a nod, opening the door.

'It's snowing!' exclaimed Nicky.

We all stared out to see a few small flakes falling from the greyness.

'It is not enough to settle,' I stated.

'Maybe it'll get thicker,' he said hopefully.

'As long as it doesn't do so before I get home,' responded Essy as she stepped out. 'Take good care,' she said in parting.

'Safe journey.'

Nicky cuddled into me as we watched her walk along the path in the gloom. She made her way out of the gate and waved in parting as she passed south. We waved back and I shut the door, barring the wind from entry and hoping the fire would soon make its warmth known.

* * *

I walked through the deepening darkness unsure of my direction. I'd only visited Chula's once before and had become lost and disorientated. The indistinct shapes of hills amidst the thickening snowfall gave no clue as to the location of her farmstead and I was filled with frustration as I walked with hands buried deep in my pockets and collar raised.

Able to make out a woodland rising up the slope of a hill to the left, I thought it may be Black Hill and hope was renewed. If I were right, then the vale and Chula's house lay on the far side.

With head bowed, I made my way towards the trees. The pain in my chest diminishing, I shivered from the penetrating cold as clouds of snow were lifted from the grassland by gusts of wind. One engulfed me as it was blown south, the flakes caressing my cheeks and the world temporarily vanishing as I was consumed.

The billowing flakes passed, the wind once more falling away as I neared the woodland and entered its relative shelter. The trunks were bars of deeper pitch against the blackness as I made my way to the foot of the hill and began the climb.

The branches rustled as a gust passed through them and I wondered if I should make my way to the south end of the hill and pass around into the bottom of the vale. My need to be with Chula was great and I chose to continue up, knowing that the passage over the hill was the quickest route to her side.

Passing between two trees, I came to a sudden halt when I felt the presence of metal beneath my boot and heard a click. I winced, expecting the jaws of the bear trap to bite at any moment.

Nothing happened.

I lowered myself, careful not to move my right foot for fear that any disturbance would close the trap. Delicately feeling about the ground, I discovered the jaws of the contraption. They had risen a few inches above the dead leaves and foliage of the woodland floor, but had halted, though whether this was due to rust or some other obstruction, I could not discern.

Looking about in the darkness, I could see no pieces of timber or rocks by which to keep the jaws open in order to make my escape. Swallowing back and feeling perspiration building beneath my arms, I straightened and heard the creak of metal as the jaws threatened to snap shut.

I stood a moment, my pulse quickening and palms becoming clammy. My muscles tensed as I prepared to leap, eyes wide as I stared into the night.

* * *

I walked out of the bedroom after checking on Nicky. He was fast asleep and the colour had returned to his cheeks since eating, an oat cake and two slices of sponge having followed the eggs.

I went to the window in the main room and stared out. Thick flakes brushed against the glass, the wind having died away to sudden gusts. 'Where are you?' I asked the night as the fire crackled behind me, feeling as though something terrible had befallen Hashi and agitated by the sensation.

Nothing could keep my thoughts from him nor cause me to settle. I wanted to go and search for him, but the doctor had been clear in his instruction not to leave Nicky unattended. My heart held me in place and at the same time yearned for me to leave, the resulting tension causing my restlessness.

'The journal!' I exclaimed as an idea struck me.

I hastened down the hall and slowed my pace as I drew up to the door. I put my palm to it and gently pushed it open, poking my head around to check that Nicky slept undisturbed.

Seeing that he was still lost to slumber, I padded into the room and went over to the chest of drawers. Opening the bottom one, I slid the journal from its resting place.

Returning to the main room, I set the leather-bound book on the table and then crouched before the dresser. Opening the cabinet doors, I squinted as I looked into the shadowy confines. Locating the ink and quill that had originally been used to write the journal and had since been used for Nicky's lessons, I took them out and went to the table.

Seating myself, I opened the book and flicked to the first blank page. Deciding to put a little distance between the previous entries and the new, I turned it over and reached for the ink pot while thinking where I should start in the telling of mine and Hashi's beginnings.

Taking off the top and picking up the quill, I dipped its tip into the ink and wiped it on the rim to clear any excess. It hovered above the page a moment as I tried to remember the date and work backwards to where I intended to start.

'Tuesday, April the eighth, 1873,' I said to myself as I began to write, hoping he would soon return and that the activity would distract my mind from the feeling that something was terribly wrong.

* * *

The journal lay open upon the tabletop as I stood at the window, the ink and quill resting nearby. Its ability to distract had diminished until I could no longer concentrate on the words.

I stared forlornly at the distorted reflection of my face which was imposed over the darkness beyond. I had finally released the past and opened my heart to the present, to a new love, but it seemed its potential was to be denied by circumstance.

Feeling as if the walls were closing in about me, I was overcome by the urge to go outside. I glanced down the hallway, sure that Nicky would be fine if I briefly left the house.

Going to the door, I put my coat of furs over the buckskin dress and britches I had changed into. Drawing it shut and holding it at the neck, I opened the door and quickly stepped out so as not to release the meagre heat that had gathered in the house.

The night was full of whispers as flakes fell thick and pale in the darkness, suddenly swirling and agitated by the wind as it gusted and I made my way to the gate. Snow crunched underfoot and the light spilling from the window illuminated the blanket that had settled upon the ground.

Leaning on the gate with my free hand, I peered into the darkness gathered in the fold of the vale. I could see nothing as flakes brushed against my cheeks and settled in my hair.

Memories of dancing at the ruined barn came to the fore as I looked south and willed Hashi to appear. That time of happiness had been brief, the joy felt by Nicholas and I soon brought to a bloody end.

'Please do not let it be brief again,' I pleaded, the mist of my breath taken on a gust of wind that lifted a cloud of soft flakes and blew them southward.

From out of their paleness appeared a figure. My heart raced as I stared at its approach. There was no evidence of a stoop and I put aside thoughts that it could be Inki returning.

'Hashi?'

'Chula?'

My heart leapt at the sound of his voice.

Opening the gate, I ran through the snow towards him. Flinging my arms about him, I held him close and was overcome by such profound thankfulness that tears immediately sprang from my eyes.

'You came back,' I stated, nestling my face into his neck.

'Where else would I go?' he asked rhetorically as he took me by the arms and gently pushed me back, looking to my face in the darkness. 'It's good to see you,' he stated, his own eyes awash with tender emotions.

'What happened?'

'It was as I thought. Bartholomew put on a performance and my brother was left with little choice other than to let me return to you.'

'You were gone so long.'

'I lost my way in the darkness,' he admitted. 'There was a bear trap, but the jaws jammed and it didn't spring shut. I was able to leap to safety,' he revealed.

'Coop,' I stated, glancing aside thoughtfully.

'What?'

I turned back to him. 'Another time,' I replied. 'I thought something awful had befallen you.'

'It nearly did.'

I shook my head and began to weep, my body trembling with the force of my feelings as the agitation of the previous hours was replaced by relief.

Hashi drew me close once again and stroked my hair. 'Chi-hollo-li,' he said softly.

The words that had so often passed my lips were finally spoken back to me. My heart broke with the beauty of the moment as the snow whispered about us and ghostly clouds of flakes passed across the night landscape.

Monday, August 25, 1873

Essy pushed Nicky as the boy sat on the swing that Hashi had made for him and I watched from the doorway of the house. My gaze moved to the barn beyond. It had become nothing more than a pile of rubble covered in foliage. What was left of the walls had fallen in soon after the last snow and now the remains of my old life were covered in new growth.

The scent of oat cakes drifted to me on the light summer breeze as I turned to find Marie taking them from the stove, heavily pregnant and with a maternal glow. 'They smell good,' I stated as she placed them on top and Nicky's laughter lifted into the air.

Brief hammering sounded from the boy's room and I glanced down the hallway. 'Should I call them through?'

'That would be a good idea,' replied Marie as she cradled the swell of her stomach. 'The coffee is ready too.'

I walked to the hall. 'Hashi. Anders. There is food and drink if you want it,' I called.

The two men soon appeared from the door on the right. They came along the short corridor, both smiling when they caught the scent of the cakes.

'Nicky will be happy,' commented Anders as he walked past me and over to the table, his wife taking down five cups.

'I'll do that,' he stated, going to her and taking over the duty of making the coffee.

Hashi came to a stop before me and I brushed some sawdust from his pale shirt.

'How is it coming?' I asked.

'We're nearly done,' he replied, looking at me with affection and gently placing his palm to my stomach. 'Our child's cradle,' he smiled, shaking his head. 'I can hardly comprehend it.'

I beamed up at him. 'Our second child,' I stated.

'Indeed,' he nodded. 'I'll call the first in,' he added, moving away from me and to the door.

'Oat cakes,' he shouted before going to the table. 'That'll bring him in quicker than anything else I could say,' he commented at he took a seat.

We all laughed and, sure enough, Nicky appeared in the doorway shortly after. He hurried to the stove and bent to the cakes, sniffing deeply.

'Mmm, they always smell so good,' he stated.

'Sit yourself down and then you can have some,' I instructed.

'Can I sit on Hashi's lap?' he requested.

I gave a nod of approval as Essy walked in, her pregnant bulge almost matching Marie's. Nicky was helped onto his desired lap and Anders passed out the coffees he had poured as Marie and Essy seated themselves at the table.

I stood and stared at the scene with tears glistening in my eyes. 'Thank you,' I whispered.

'Will you be joining us, Chula?' asked Hashi with a smile as Nicky reached for the tray of oat cakes that Anders had placed in the centre of the table.

I smiled back at him and walked over. Pulling out the last seat, I sat with my family and looked to Nicky, knowing that you were with us too.

Afterward

It took 21 days to write the first draft of *Snow Dancer* and I enjoyed returning to Chula in order to discover what would happen in her life. I already knew I wanted this book to be the positive to the negative of *Savage*, and so also knew that the journey wouldn't be as gruelling as it was with that book.

I envisioned the books as being akin to the yin-yang symbol. *Snow Dancer* was therefore to be the yang to the yin of *Savage*. Just as the yin contains a small amount of light, so did *Savage*. This came in the form of the love between Chula and Nicholas, along with the brief happiness they shared and the birth of their son at the end. Therefore, to create the balance, there had to be an element of dark in *Snow Dancer*. This mainly arose in relation to Chula and Hashi's pasts, to which each clung to some degree. It was also apparent in relation to the reactions of their close families.

Hopefully this yin-yang relationship between the two books is apparent and you have reached the end of *Snow Dancer* feeling uplifted. During the writing process, there were a number of occasions when I experienced joy or heartfelt empathy, not least when Hashi and Chula go to his house for the first time and are both overcome by emotion.

Hashi was actually a surprising addition to the story. When Chula first went to visit with Essy, I had no idea they would be forced to conduct this meeting in the granary. Essy then naturally gave her sister the grain and it became apparent that the sack was torn. Realising that someone would see the grain leaking out, I thought it would be Akocha who brought Chula's attention to it, having already anticipated his arrival in the story. However, it was Hashi, and until he appeared, I had no idea he'd be in the book nor that the narrative would essentially be a love story. This obviously completely changed my perception of *Snow Dancer* and created a second strand to the journal entries which I had not foreseen.

The primary theme of the book is new life. This not only relates to pregnancy and birth, but to releasing the past and living in the present. Both Chula and Hashi hold on to elements of their past. Through their interactions, their wish to cling on is revealed for what it is and they are able to break the bonds they have formed with what has been in order to embrace what is and the potential this holds.

Snow Dancer is the seventh I have written in the group of titles I term my 'slave books,' the fourth and final of the *Runaway Series* already completed, though not due for release until June of this year. All of them, along with my other three historical novels set in western Cornwall, England, tell the stories of people who are outcasts in one way or another. This is more direct in *Savage* and *Snow Dancer* than in any of the others because of Chula's status.

These titles thereby encourage us to be more accepting. They show that judging by appearances is flawed and that we should not seek to condemn, but to understand. It is also the case that I identify with the outcast characters. This is because I feel as though I am on the periphery of society, with an unusual job and 'alternative' lifestyle. In a sense, this makes me an outcast and the books could also be seen as my own plea not to be judged, but to be accepted for who I am, rather than what I look like or how I live.

It may also be worth mentioning the weather while writing this book as it was coincidentally apt considering the title. During the writing of the first draft, the area in which I live had its heaviest snowfall in 32 years (a couple of inches). Then, during the editorial process, it snowed again. I have lived here for 12 years and only seen snow five times previous, and never to such an extent due to this region being mild and coastal. It is also quite rare to have snow in March and the first fall gave me the opportunity to go out with my camera and experience the landscape for myself, walking through fields as the gusting wind picked up clouds of snow, something which was then woven into the conclusion of the story.

Something else that helped set the tone of this book was the film *The New World*. Written and directed by Terrence Mallick, it is based on fact. A love story between a Native American and an English settler in what is now called Virginia, it is the true story of Pocahontas. Both thoughtful and engaging, this movie was played regularly during the writing process, along with others and a specific playlist of music.

As far as historical data goes, there is nothing new to share here as all relevant information was given at the end of *Savage*. However, the dates in the book correspond to the correct days of the week for 1873 and there really was a full moon on the night of April 11.

It is also the case that records of snowfall in the Oklahoma area have been compiled using data going back to 1893. At that time, Oklahoma did not exist as a state as it was established as the 46th state of the Union on November 16, 1907. These records show that the latest snowfall occurred on April 30 in both 1907 and 1949. The latest measurable snowfall fell on April 12, 1957 and was 0.7 inches. In the book, which is set before records began, the snow also falls on April 12 and is therefore within the bounds of reality.

Thank you for reading *Snow Dancer* and I hope that it has had a positive impact. May the tracks you leave behind reveal you to be a person of compassion and beauty.

Publisher's Note: *The Shack on the Hill* is the eighth title in what the author terms his 'slave books' and is due for release on 25th August 2018 in both Kindle and paperback formats. The former will be available for pre-order from the 1st of that month.

If you enjoyed reading *Snow Dancer*, then try the author's other novels relating to slavery during the time of the Civil War, including the *Runaway Series*. Alternatively, try his three historical novels set in western Cornwall, England. Entitled *Where Seagulls Fly* (2013 Edition), *Song of the Sea* and *The Shepherd of St Just*, each tells the emotive tale of an outcast.

Made in the USA
Columbia, SC
02 February 2022